# ICONIC
# RHODE ISLAND
## An ARIA Anthology

**Selected short fiction, nonfiction, poetry & prose
from The Association of Rhode Island Authors**

# Previous ARIA Anthologies

# Table of Contents

# Introduction

The theme for this year's ARIA anthology is "Iconic Rhode Island." Now, if you're a Rhode Islander, by birth or otherwise, there are probably a variety of things that come to mind when you read those words: chowder and clam cakes, Benny's, the Big Blue Bug, coffee milk, Almacs, Del's….the list goes on.

We asked our writers to consider the theme and interpret it in their own way. And the result? A wonderful batch of stories and poems that reflect the many ways we see our little state.

There are memories, to be sure, of the Blizzard of '78, minor league baseball games, and carefree summer days spent by the ocean, but our writers also bent the rule a bit by setting a murder at one of Rhode Island's better known "gentlemen's" establishments, a fantastic homage to Rhode Island's own H.P. Lovecraft, and a ride along the beautiful East Bay bike path.

Enjoy this volume at your leisure! I think you'll find it's the perfect book to pick up when you need to escape, whether into another time, a favorite place, or a distant memory. Our Rhode Island authors have done Rhode Island proud.

Many thanks to the panel of five judges, who devoted two months in 2022 to reading and reviewing each submission.

Your purchase of this volume helps the Association of Rhode Island Authors continue its work of educating and promoting local writers. Thank you!

*Martha Reynolds*

Chair, 2022 ARIA Anthology
Association of Rhode Island Authors

# Iconic Rhode Island

# The Lamassu

*by Paul Magnan*

The saturnine man frowned at the unexpected knock at his door. Undoubtedly one of his students, looking to beg for more time on a project. They were working with clay, not stone or metal. How much more time did they need?

"Enter!" He said, his voice gruff and unwelcoming.

The door opened. Instead of a student, two middle-aged men in dark suits entered. The man behind the desk sat straighter.

One of the men, short and bespeckled, spoke. "Hello, George. May we sit?"

George Brewster nodded. "Of course, gentlemen! Please take a seat."

The visitors sat in well-worn chairs. Each wore a gold ring, with a black pearl set in the center, on their right index fingers. George rested his right hand on the cherrywood desk. His finger bore the same type of ring. "You grace me with your presence. May I inquire as to the nature of your business?"

The taller of the two, a black man with bushy sideburns, leaned forward. "I'm afraid the time is nigh. The auguries foretell the arrival of the Herald."

George Brewster drew in a breath. "What auspices have been seen?"

"A red moon rises above the ocean," the shorter man said. "And throughout the night whip-poor-wills flap their dark wings, then sing their songs of death within patches of blackthorn."

Ice gripped George's heart. "If the Herald has indeed been born, I must start immediately."

Both men nodded. "How long will it take to create the lamassu?"

"It will take at least five years, and I will need money for the bronze and gold leaf."

"How much money will the work require?"

1

"I am thinking three thousand dollars. I know that is much, my friends."

"We will provide the funds," the taller man said.

"Of course, I will need to resign my post here."

"The Rhode Island School of Design will carry on without you," the shorter man said. "Humanity, however, cannot."

George Brewster rose and came around the desk. His visitors rose with him. All three held out their right hands. The black pearls on each ring touched.

They spoke in unison. "The Apkallu R'lyeh watches and keeps the Old One in eternal slumber."

Sam Brewster stood on the sidewalk off Smith Street. Cars and SUVs zipped by with no regard to speed limits or traffic lights. Some came so close to the curb that Sam felt the sudden breeze on the back of his trousers. He ignored it.

He looked over the large concourse, decorated with fifteen red squares, that fronted the north side of the majestic Rhode Island State House. Built with white Georgian marble, its classical style featured a center dome, which was the fourth largest unsupported dome in the world.

On a pedestal at the crown of the dome stood a bronze statue, clad in gold leaf. It was a man, bare but for a fur pelt around his waist, with a long-shafted spear in his right hand. His left hand rested on an anchor, the prominent symbol of Rhode Island. The colossus was eleven feet in height and weighed five hundred pounds. The statue was called by most the Independent Man.

Sam Brewster referred to it by another name: Hope. This was also the motto of Rhode Island, and the original name given to the statue by its creator, George Brewster, Sam's great-grandfather. The statue was George Brewster's legacy to the city and state that had been his home for a remarkably short period of time.

Sam Brewster looked down at his right hand. On his index finger was a heavy gold ring, set with a black pearl in its center. This was his legacy from his ancestor, one that carried an onerous burden.

He saw her approaching but said nothing until she stopped by his side. Her hair was long and shockingly white, her skin smooth and dark. On her right hand was a gold ring with a black pearl. Sam turned and was not surprised to see depths of trepidation in her brown eyes.

"Hi, Janelle."

Janelle's features tightened. "Is that all you can say? 'Hi, Janelle'?"

"What do you want me to say?"

Janelle shook her head and looked at the State House. "Have you seen what's been written in every part of the city? Even private homes have been marked. The Followers are massing." She turned back to Sam. "Black wax and slaughtered animals have been found at the Herald's gravesite. The rituals have begun. They seek to awaken..." Janelle shuddered, unable to finish.

"It. I know." Sam had seen the graffiti, of course. Six words, from a language never spoken by man, adorned buildings in every sector of the city.

Sam corrected himself. Only five of the words were alien. The original script, written by the Herald nearly a century ago, had been altered.

"Ph'nglui mglw'nafh Cthulhu Providence wgah'nagl fhtagn." Which meant, "In his house

below Providence, dead Cthulhu waits dreaming." The original writing made no mention of Rhode Island's capital city. In his fevered state, the Herald had identified the Old One's home as R'lyeh, located somewhere in the South Pacific. After the Herald died in 1937, his followers dedicated their lives to travelling the world and amassing chthonic grimoires in their pursuit of dark knowledge. These corrupted souls were known as Cuthah Irra, or "Dedicates of He Who Brings Annihilation."

Sam and Janelle turned as a police vehicle pulled to the curb. A Providence police sergeant with close-cropped, graying hair and wearing glasses, stepped out and nodded to them. "Sam, Janelle."

"Hi, Stuart," Sam said.

Stuart came right to the point. "Has the time come?" He folded his right hand over his left. On his right index finger was the same ring that Sam and Janelle wore. "What does the Necronomicon say?"

The Necronomicon, the oldest and most potent of the chthonic grimoires, was acquired by Sam's great-grandfather, George Brewster, in 1891. Like the ring he wore, it had been passed down through the generations. Sam had read and memorized it, at the cost of endless nightmares.

3

Sam's eyes found the sidewalk. "You have found evidence of two conjuration rituals, correct?"

"Yeah, the first in the parking lot behind the business on Angell Street."

"Where the Herald's birth home once stood," Janelle said.

Stuart nodded. "The second being at Swan's Point, where he is buried. At both locations we found black candle stubs and eviscerated cats."

Janelle looked at Sam. "And of course, cats were the Herald's favored creatures."

"Yes, they were sacred to him, the killing of which could only bring about evil." Sam cleared his throat. "Two rituals have been performed. They need to do one more."

"Where?" Stuart asked.

Sam was silent a moment. "The churchyard."

Janelle and Stuart were silent. Sam held out his ring hand, as did the others. The three black pearls touched.

"The Apkallu R'lyeh watches and keeps the Old One in eternal slumber."

The hands separated. Janelle looked at the State House.

"What of the lamassu?"

Sam sighed. "If it comes to that, it may already be too late."

The graveyard behind St. John's church on North Main Street, even late at night, was not entirely dark; light from the capital city gave the grounds a dull luminescence. It was enough to show the three individuals that they were the only living people there.

Stuart held his service handgun and flashlight together as he scanned behind every tombstone. Except for moths and crickets, he found nothing.

"Are you sure this is the location of the third ritual?" Janelle asked Sam.

"I'm certain of it. This cemetery held high significance for the Herald." Sam sounded certain, though in truth doubt had sunk its claws into him. If he was wrong about this…

"Hey, we might have something here."

Stuart's flashlight shone on a tomb built within an earthen berm. The tomb was made of stone blocks, several of which were loose. A weathered wooden door, set within an arch, was ajar.

With Stuart in the lead, the three approached the tomb. He kept his gun trained and nodded to Sam to pull the door open. The wood had expanded over the years, but Sam, after a couple of tugs, opened the door the rest of the way.

The tomb was empty of life. Between two sarcophagi was a cleared circle, around which were several black candle stubs and the remains of a flayed cat. On the back wall, written in the cat's blood, was a message: *The Great One will rise and swallow the sun. Woe to you, Apkallu R'lyeh, and the sacrificial beasts that are humanity.*

Stuart hissed. "Damn it. Now what?"

Sam looked out the open doorway. In the east, the sky had turned gray with the coming dawn.

The earth began to shake. "We need to get to the State House, now."

It started as tremors but soon developed into earth-splitting convulsions that uprooted trees and sent buildings crumbling to the ground. Panic thickened the air as people screamed and sought shelter that was nonexistent. Cars trucks, busses, and trains got tossed like toys, and some were swallowed in massive crevices that suddenly opened beneath them. Bridges swayed, then collapsed over the Providence and Seekonk rivers, sending dozens of vehicles to the turbulent waters. The junction of the rivers rose and inundated South and East Providence. A great wall of brackish water swept over the Fox Point Hurricane Barrier and surged through the downtown area, sweeping away cars, businesses, and people.

Sam, Janelle, and Stuart stood in the center of the concourse before the State House. They were a center of calm amidst the chaos of the city. Fires burned unchecked around them, darkening the sky with smoke. The quakes lessened, then finally stopped.

Except for car and fire alarms, the city was silent. Everyone stilled, as if in disbelief of what had happened, and in dread anticipation of what might be coming next.

The upper part of Narragansett Bay bubbled and steamed. A monstrous green head rose from the surface. Throughout the city, those that had survived the horrors of the earthquake looked on in shock as the alien creature, impossibly huge, continued to rise. Two cephalopod eyes emerged, glowing with an eldritch light that seemed to see and mark every soul within the city. Below those merciless eyes, long, thick tentacles writhed to the surface. One wrapped around a cargo ship and dragged it under the waves. Another tore through a massive oil tank and set it ablaze. Black smoke blotted out the sun.

Terror shot through the city as those who had been stunned by the appearance of the monster now ran screaming from it.

"Hail, Cthulhu, Lord of all! We, the Cuthah Irra, welcome you!"

Sam and the others spun around. Three men and two women, dressed in black robes, were on their knees at the edge of the concourse. The nearest, a tall, thin man, turned to them.

"You are too late, Apkallu R'lyeh! The Dark Lord has risen! He has consumed the sun, and soon he will consume you."

"You idiots!" Janelle yelled at them. "That thing will consume you, too."

"No, we shall be exalted!" The robed man looked at the beast. "The Great One sees us. We shall be placed above you all!"

Even from this distance, the baleful eyes seemed to focus on them. One of the tentacles shot forward and stretched over the miles. It reached the State House and coiled above the robed figures, who smiled with expectant ecstasy. The underside of the mottled appendage had massive suckers, from which sprouted sharp, bony hooks. Dripping toxic slime, the limb whipped around the Cuthah Irra and drew back. The five worshippers were thrust into a gaping red maw under the squirming mass.

"So much for being exalted," Stuart said.

"Enough," Sam said. "We need to stop this, now."

The Apkallu R'lyeh faced the State House and raised their arms. Their ring fingers faced the eleven-foot statue at the top of the dome.

The Independent Man. Hope.

"Inlil aleazim," They chanted. "Aladhi tasjud 'amamah alihat al-zalam khwfan, asmae salatina. Amnah allaamasu alhayat lihazimat aleajuza. Amnah allaamasw ehdan liantasir qabl alrahbat kuthulihi." Mighty Enlil, before whom the dark gods bow down in fear, hear our prayer. Give the lamassu life to defeat the Old One. Give the lamassu triumph over dread Cthulhu.

The dark smoke that obscured the sky burst open and a ray of sunlight bathed the figure atop the State House. Booming cracks echoed across the concourse as the Independent Man freed one foot, then the other, from its pedestal. With a groan of metal, the statue turned its head and looked down at the Apkallu R'lyeh. Its eyes shone with the power of the sun.

The lamassu created by George Brewster more than a century earlier shot into the air. It followed the path of the life-giving sun, spear in one hand and anchor in the other. Though it seemed tiny compared to Cthulhu, the beast saw the lamassu and roared, a sonic blast that crumpled nearby structures. The Dark One's tentacles flayed as the bronze figure flew over it. The Independent Man knocked one of the massive appendages away with the spear, opening a smoking gash in the gelatinous flesh.

The bronze icon reached the top of Cthulhu's head. Still flying within the golden sunlight, the Independent Man lowered the spear's blade and sliced through the rubbery skin, creating a pattern that the three Apkallu R'lyeh could not see. A giant arm exploded from the bay and a webbed claw swiped at the statue. The Independent Man flew beyond its reach.

The pattern that the spear had carved expanded and opened. Sickly orange light emanated from the wound, which now revealed itself to be an eight-pointed star with a triangle in its center. Cthulhu bellowed again, the unearthly sound knocking Sam, Janelle, and Stuart off their feet. The Old One loosed another arm from the water and reached for its tormentor.

The lamassu, encased in its solar protection, cast the spear at the beast. The blade struck the center of the star and disappeared within the triangle.

The shriek that tore from the Dark God blasted remaining buildings within a mile to dust. Sam covered his ears as the sound sent white-hot blades into his brain. Janelle and Stuart writhed in pain on the ground. Sam forced himself to turn back to the cosmic battle.

The only thing not affected was the Independent Man, who kept out of reach of Cthulhu's claws and tentacles. Even from several miles away Sam saw the pure, cleansing light blazing from the lamassu's eyes. Armed only with the anchor, it dove with incredible speed toward its gargantuan enemy. The anchor struck the pulsating lesion in the center of the triangle. It sank into the cavity and the Independent Man, celestially bright, followed.

Sam stood in shock. The lamassu, gone? Had Cthulhu won?

The dire glow of the great beast's eyes dimmed. Its arms and tentacles fell limp. Black waves flooded the blasted land as the huge body convulsed. Blisters grew on the mucilaginous skin and burst, spreading viscous orange fluid over the Dark One's body. Its claws tore at its tentacled face as more blisters formed and ruptured. Cthulhu shuddered and dissolved, its bloated form collapsing on itself like a punctured balloon. The remains of the gigantic horror slipped beneath the roiling surface of Narragansett Bay.

The three Apkallu R'lyeh, choking from the stench of Cthulhu's sizzling flesh, looked up and saw they were not alone. Thousands of Providence residents surrounded the State House, staring with astonishment at the empty place where the beloved Independent Man had stood for decades.

"Is it over?" Janelle asked. "Did the lamassu destroy Cthulhu?"

Stuart cleared his throat. "We all saw what happened. Cthulhu is dead."

Sam shook his head. "Cthulhu is not dead, it is death. The Dark One is not of this universe. The laws of mortality don't apply to it. Remember the words of the Herald: 'Dead Cthulhu waits dreaming.' We cannot kill it, only drive it back into cosmic slumber."

Stuart looked at him in shock. "You mean Cthulhu is going to return?"

"Yes. It is inevitable. There will always be those who take the Herald's word as gospel, like those unfortunate, misguided Cuthah Irra. It may not happen in our lifetime, or for several generations to come, but it will happen."

Janelle's face hardened. "What can we do to drive it back to its beauty sleep when it does rise again?"

Sam looked up to the empty pedestal on the State House dome. "Along with this ring and the Necronomicon, my great-grandfather's artistic notes were handed down to me."

Realization dawned in Stuart and Janelle. "You mean to create another lamassu?"

Sam gave them a grim smile. "Did you think the Independent Man was the first lamassu to be created? This struggle has been going on for thousands of years. It will continue for as long as Cthulhu directs its hunger to the human souls of this world. Lamassus are the tools used by Enlil, the Mesopotamian divinity we now simply call "God," to keep the Dark One in check and the cosmos from obliteration."

Sam paused, then continued. "Though it will tax your sanity and possibly damage your souls, you both need to read the Necronomicon so you can assist me in creating a new vessel to house Enlil's will. Only in that way will we preserve our world."

Janelle and Stuart stood firm. "The Apkallu R'lyeh watches and keeps the Old One in eternal slumber."

ᱷ

*For Howard Phillips Lovecraft, the "Herald" of Rhode Island horror.*

**Paul Magnan** has been writing stories that veer from the straight and narrow for many years. He has had short stories published in Fantasy Scroll Magazine, Sanitarium Magazine, The Horror Zine, and several other venues, including previous ARIA anthologies. He has a short story in the anthology *Violent Vixens: An Homage to Grindhouse Horror*, published by Dark Peninsula Press. His short story collection, *Veering from the Straight and Narrow*, is available on Amazon, as is his dark fantasy series, *Kyu, The Unknown*. He lives with his family in the wilds of Rhode Island.

# The Ferris Wheel at Rocky Point

(written as the park neared its end)
*by Roberta Mudge Humble*

Rough surface in salty air.
Great trees, symmetrical twins,
Swing in the symphony of seats
and towering trusses.
Showered by storm,
Squeaking sequentially,
Rocking relentlessly.

A lonely peninsula —
An agonizing, suffering spirit,
Wrestling with reminiscence,
Writhing in rainy tears.

The solitary silent wheel,
Languishes in loneliness,
Emptied of excitement,
Dreading defining demise, Steely in the rain.

But then powerful reflections
Of sweet, blissful moments —
Of pleasure so very unforgotten —
Of grandest affection never lost —
Rise, touch, and soothe.

ଓଃ

**Roberta Mudge Humble** rarely writes poetry. She has written seven books and created seven games – all about Rhode Island – and gives twelve rousing presentations on Rhode Island with glorious pictures of all parts of the state. She is a retired CCRI professor where she taught Technical Writing for 47 years. Her passion is historic armories. She is president of the Westerly Armory which has an event venue in its drill hall, a museum of both military and community memorabilia, and a home for the Westerly Band. Her best-known books are *The RIght to Crow* and *The Historic Armories of Rhode Island.* The recipient of many state and national awards, she was inducted into the Rhode Island Heritage Hall of Fame in 2022. And she adores birds.

# It Took a Village, a City, and a State
# The Blizzard of 1978

*by Pam Carey*

The snow began mid-morning Monday, February 6. Although it was heavy and wet, I wasn't too concerned. It was a typical mid-winter scenario in Rhode Island and forecasters hadn't predicted anything extraordinary. Our pantry shelves always contained gallons of water, boxes of milk (which the kids wouldn't touch!), cereals, bread, crackers, peanut butter and jelly, applesauce, canned tuna, peas, and fruits, mayonnaise, toilet paper, and dog food, in addition to the boys' favorite pastas, spaghetti sauces, and mac-and-cheeses. In Rhode Island there was always a chance the power could go out, winter or summer.

Tim and Todd, ages six and seven, had trudged off, as usual, to the bus stop at 8:00 a.m. at the top of the incline that led to our cul-de-sac; Charley had driven to work in Providence, which normally took twenty minutes. They'd all worn enough gear to camp out in the Arctic.

That left me with our Airedale, Sandy. I sat in my office placing orders for clients' fabrics and furniture and lost track of time. Sandy was out cold under my feet.

Around 1:30 I stopped for some yogurt and tea. The wind was howling, but the oil burner was cranking up its hot water, and the disgruntled pipes were grunting. Outside, flakes swirled in demented patterns and our driveway had disappeared. I turned on the television.

Some superintendents around the state had let their schools out early, but not in Cumberland. I heard a new forecast. "We're in the middle of an Arctic cold front" (no kidding?) "that has merged with an extratropical cyclone off South Carolina, creating intense low pressure. A Canadian high-pressure system has stalled and may keep the cold front from moving off the coast. Please remain off the roads as much as possible."

My boys – where were they? If the roads were getting impassable and the buses weren't running, were they stranded at school? I called the office at Community School. No answer. I called a neighbor. "Diane, have you heard anything about the schools closing?"

"I haven't heard a word. Our kids should be getting on the bus about now. Do you have some supplies and flashlights?"

"Yes, we're all set. Let me know if you hear or need anything. Thanks."

Outside my office windows the accumulation was beginning to creep up the lamppost. Back in front of the television, I heard, "The storm may intensify with accumulations of up to four inches an hour. Because of the new moon, there may be unusually high tides."

We had a beach house in nearby Westport, Massachusetts, but thankfully, it wasn't directly on the water. Where the hell were my sons? They were usually home by this time. I called Charley.

"Honey, the snow is accumulating fast and the kids aren't home yet!"

"Well, the buses are probably having trouble. It's only two-thirty, and that's when they normally get home, isn't it? Don't panic yet."

"I don't think the bus will make it down our street. The snow's already six inches up our lamppost. When are you coming home?"

"I've got a meeting at four in my office and then I'll head out. By the way, we were supposed to get an oil delivery this week, so keep an eye on the gauge in the basement."

"I'll check it now. Maybe you'd better think about cancelling and start home."

"We'll see. Love you."

"Love you, too! Please leave as soon as possible."

I raced down the basement steps to check the oil gauge. The black line floated in the lower section of the tube at one-quarter full. I ran back up to the kitchen and looked up the oil company's number. No answer there, but their voicemail was on. "This is Mrs. Carey on Lantern Lane in Cumberland. We're on an automatic delivery plan and our tank is registering one-quarter full. Please refill our tank as soon as possible! My number is ----------."

I called Diane again. "Diane, there's no answer at the school. If the kids aren't home by three-thirty, I think we should try to get there. Do you want me to pick you up?"

"Pam, I don't see how you're going to make it. There must be six inches on the ground already. Hopefully, they'll be home any minute."

I hung up and started to pull on my knee-high, lined after-ski boots. I could at least hike to the top of our street and perhaps see the bus. That's when I heard the garage door go up beneath the family room. I flung the boots off and ran to the basement stairs (again).

"Oh, thank heavens you're home!" I yelled, grabbing each son as he came into the kitchen. Cakes of white melted into puddles on the floor.

"Yeah, we all had to get out and push the bus so it could turn around. The driver wouldn't come down our street and the rest of the kids have to call their parents at the Lynches' house to come get them."

"Well, you made it! Why don't you leave your wet things in the basement and I'll make some hot chocolate? Your dad's still in Providence."

"Is he coming home?"

"As soon as he can get away from the bank."

…Which wasn't soon enough. "Honey, the kids got home! I think you should leave right now," I warned Charley.

"I'll be leaving in about half an hour. Did you call the oil company?"

"Yes, but I had to leave a message. They're usually good about refilling the tank, but there's no-one picking up their messages. Stay safe!"

At 4:30 I called Charley again at his office. No answer. Maybe he was on his way?

At 5:00 I tried again. This time he picked up. "Are you still at work?" I sounded panicky, which I was.

"Yeah, 'fraid so. I got my car out of the municipal lot and started home but didn't get very far. All the roads in the city are blocked by stalled cars. I left mine on the side of South Main Street."

"What are you going to do?'

"Sleep on the couch in my office, I guess."

At least he was safe, while the electricity held. "How are you going to eat?"

"The café on the first floor is staying open. The owner is a real stand-up guy. I guess he got stranded, too."

By the next day, the café's customers had eaten every chunk of meat in the establishment. Mabel in the Accounting Department was stuck

14

in her office and was one of the owner's favorites. Everyone eyeing a piece of chocolate cake in the café was out of luck. The cake had disappeared into Accounting. Charley was subsisting on bagels and cream cheese.

In the morning, I went downstairs to let the dog out. The front door was blocked shut. Blown snow had turned into a wall of ice as high as our second story and was pushing against the door. The snow hadn't stopped but had become lighter, powdery. I got a shovel from the garage and cracked chunks from around the door to wedge it open a foot. Then I chipped away a tunnel as far as the shovel would reach. Good thing Sandy was small for her breed! She was out and in again within two minutes, backing up because she couldn't turn around. I cleaned off the excrement from her paws with a rag. At least the wind had died down.

"Is this the last jug of milk?" Tim asked at breakfast.

"Yes, but we have the boxes," I said. "Maybe they'll plow later and we can get out." Tim's scrunched up nose and told me he and his brother wouldn't be trying the boxed milk.

I called Charley's office. "How did you sleep?"

"Well, I can't complain with a couch in my office. Some of the guys had to sleep in their chairs. The power's still on and I got some juice downstairs. My breath smells like a sewer, but so does everyone else's. If I'm stuck here another day, my underwear will stand up by itself."

"Don't you move till they clear the roads! We never lost power here, so we're fine. I'm going to try to reach the oil company again later."

I called Diane. "Did Ron make it home?"

"Yes, but did you hear about Norm, across the street? He had to leave his car on Tingley Lane and tried to cut through the woods in his backyard. The snow was up to his chest and he started to collapse. Stephanie and the kids had to go out and drag him in. Good thing she had the floodlight on or he might have been buried!"

"Speaking of buried, there must be a car buried in our driveway because all I can see from the family room is an antenna."

"Yeah, Doris next door said Art had to abandon it at the end of your driveway and walk down to their house. I'm surprised he made it."

I tried the oil company again. No answer. I recorded the same message and turned on the television. Winds had been recorded during the night at 86 miles/hour, with gusts to 111 miles/hour. I'd taken two aspirins and hadn't heard a thing.

Like a hurricane, the Nor'easter had an eye. Cumberland was in its bullseye. "The area around Cumberland and Lincoln is going to get a glimpse of sunshine today, but don't be fooled. You'll be in the center of the storm. Lightning and thunder have been recorded on the other side. Helicopters report thousands of cars are trapped in drifts along Route 128. Don't abandon your cars – REPEAT – don't abandon your cars! If you turn on your engines every hour for warmth, dig a trench behind the tail-pipe first." By the end of the storm, fourteen people had succumbed to fumes from idling engines along Route 95.

Knowing Charley was safe and still had electricity in Providence, I called neighbor Doris. "Do you have enough supplies for all seven of you?"

"For now, and thank god the electricity hasn't gone out! I heard a report they're bringing in payloaders from upstate New York to plow us out when the snow stops."

"How are they going to get here? By space ship?"

"The report said they're going to arrive at Logan (Airport) from Fort Bragg and Fort Devens. I don't know when they'll get to us, but they've got to get those poor people out of their cars on the highways. Fans at the Beanpot (Hockey Tournament) have been stuck in the Boston Garden for two days."

"I heard the Charles River is frozen over, too. I'm glad you're all safe. I'll check in with you later."

By late afternoon, the other side of the storm had flung itself to sea and the sun had appeared. Lonely swirling flakes were the only signs of the ferocity of the night before. Frozen surfaces threw glare in mirror-like patterns, hallucinatory images everywhere. A total of fifty-four inches had fallen during thirty-three hours in Cumberland.

I began working outside the garage doors to chisel a path toward the street. Tim and Todd used their kids' shovels to dispose of the chunks I left behind, but most of the remnants they threw toward the snowbanks came clunking back down. Around 4:00 p.m., we heard heavy machinery approaching. There were payloaders coming down the street as tall as our second floor, pushing aside the white mass like the prow of a battleship in turbulent seas.

With the street eventually plowed, I turned on the floodlight in the shadows facing the driveway. Teens from our cul-de-sac had put on their skis and were flying down submerged layers of ice from the top of the street, jumping over the 15-foot mound payloaders had created over the

16

hidden Rinaldi car. In New England, kids learned early how to carve their edges into the crusts.

Doris reported a shortage of bread in her house with the five kids. "Now that the street's been plowed, why don't you and the kids bring your food supplies over around 6:30? I'll invite my end of the street and we can share what we've got. My boys can shovel Art's car out."

The most common "supply" that appeared that evening at Doris and Art's was wine of every vintage and origin. In Providence, Charley tried cream cheese with chives on toast for a change of pace. "I'm taking off tomorrow morning," he told me on the phone, "even if I have to walk to Cumberland. I stink and I'm sick of cream cheese. I'll call you when I leave."

"Where's your car?"

"It got towed when the plows came through. Everything from this side of the city was put in a parking lot at Brown University. There's so much snow the only place to dump it is into the Moshassuck River. I'm going to have to pay a fine when I retrieve it – can you believe that?"

"Well, we'll deal with the car when the time comes. Get a good night's sleep and don't take any foolish chances. Call me before you leave tomorrow. I love you."

On the morning of February 8, we got a new supply of heating oil. The sun shone all day, creating icicles that hung from our roof to the ground. Around 4:00 in the afternoon, a lone figure arose like a mirage from the glare on the driveway. He lifted each leg high along the partially shoveled path, as if in drills on a football field. A dark, three-day beard covered his face; his ski beanie resembled the white whipped topping on a wedding cake; the tails of his scarf, tucked beneath his parka, created a snowman's torso; mid-calf laces on his leather boots were frozen in place. Without even grabbing a jacket, I ran down the basement stairs and heaved the garage door up.

"Thank god you made it!" I mumbled, my words lost in his stiff woolen scarf, my arms wrapped around his parka. Sugar-cubes of snow clung to my sweater. His breath was a prophylactic for any welcoming kiss, but he lunged in, anyway. Dark half-moons lay beneath his eyes. "How did you get here?"

"A guy named Ted and I caught a ride in a snowplow from Providence to Pawtucket. When I got off, I walked up Route 95 till a skimobile gave me a lift along Route 1 and up Nate Whipple Highway to the Cumberland line. The roads had been plowed so I walked the rest of the way."

"You must be starving! Let's get you out of this gear and into a shower. I made some chicken soup and I'll whip up some omelets."

"I'll eat anything but bagels and cream cheese! At least I wasn't as bad off as the guy I met, Ted. He was stuck in Girl Scout Headquarters for three days. He said he never wants to look at another Girl Scout cookie in his life!"

&#x2683;

**Pamela Carey** taught high school English in Connecticut, Georgia, and Maine, before opening her own interior design firm.

In 2009 Barking Cat Books published *Minor League Mom: A Mother's Journey through the Red Sox Farm Teams*, which became a finalist in the Royal Palm Nonfiction awards for the Florida Writer's Association. *Minor League Mom* is the story of Pam's two sons playing professional baseball for the Red Sox organization through the six levels of the minor leagues, without ever reaching the majors.

In 2014 Barking Cat Books published *Elderly Parents with All Their Marbles: A Survival Guide for the Kids*. The book won the Gold Medal in the "Self-Help" Category from the Florida Authors and Publishers Association in 2015. It is structured around 49 humorous "rules" Pam devised while navigating through her parents' healthy, independent 80s and 90s, as well as the last three months of their lives. Both of Pam's books are part of the Palm Beach County (Fl.) Local Authors Collection. She has appeared on a panel for the Writer's Colony in Delray Beach, and was chosen for the Delray Beach Library's Author's Showcase in 2009 and 2015. She has been interviewed on NPR radio, as well as on Fox TV and ABC TV, both in Providence, R.I.

In 2018 Barking Cat Books published *Surviving Your Dream Vacation: 75 Rules to Keep Your Companion Talking to You on the Road*. The book consists of chapters ranging from "Accommodations" to "Visiting Friends and Relatives," with humorous "rules" and anecdotes based on Pam's travels with her husband around the world. Pam's essays have appeared in four anthologies published by the Association of Rhode Island Authors.

When not reading, writing, or traveling, Pam can be found on the tennis court. She and her husband reside in Delray Beach, Florida, and in Westport, Massachusetts.

# At the Sign of the Golden Cow

*by L.A. Jacob*

**F**illio switched off the buttons on the console of his ship, sat back in the navigator/captain's chair, cast his head against the headrest, and closed his eyes after a relatively rough docking sequence.

"Docking complete," stated the robotic, somewhat female voice. "Please exit at your leisure. Welcome to the Truck Stop."

Fillio grumbled and unbuckled his restraints, needing to stoop to get out of the area. He couldn't stretch to his full seven-foot height until he jumped down into the cargo hold area.

He had nothing special in the hold: a few bits of luxury for some of the Goldilocks' planets nearby. Not quite a merchant or a trader, Fillio considered himself a delivery unit. Someone ordered these items for themselves; it was only natural that others on the planet would want the same thing. So, he brought a few extra, just in case.

Fillio gathered his overnight bag. The station would have places for sleeping, maybe an ionic shower, or something fresh to eat.

He exited the cargo hold into the chill of the ship's holding bay. He should have brought a jacket. But the less he carried onto the station, the less he had to keep track of. He nodded to the robot at the front.

"Are there any repairs necessary to your ship?"

"Don't touch it." Fillio peeked his head past the robot. "Food."

"The nearest food court is spinward, Red sector."

Fillio hitched the bag over his shoulder and followed the directions. The black hole the station sat next to was on his left; the center hub of the rotating round station to his right.

He paused at the gift shop. Tiny scale models of the station, t-shirts for multiple-armed and -legged creatures filled the window. The robot behind the counter used a duster to push aside the silver motes that settled on some of the merchandise.

Fillio refused to get caught up in that tourist trap, so he continued to the food court. He walked slowly by the storefronts, inhaling the scents of the different food vendors. He saw a green sign with a gold bovine on it.

*Perfect*, he thought, and he entered the establishment. The smell of humans and other creatures overpowered his sense of smell at first. Humans sat at the counter, while others lounged in booths. He was too big to fit in the booth. He was disappointed that this was yet another restaurant that catered to the smaller size of the ever-present humans.

As soon as he sat at the counter, the human waitress poured hot dark liquid into a cup before him and set down a menu in Standard. He said, in his own bad Standard, "Where am I?"

The waitress blinked. "Um, you don't know?"

He pointed to the picture, then patted his hairy bare chest. "Like me."

The waitress looked at the longhorns on his head.

"We don't serve cows here. Well, we do. Hamburgers?"

Fillio's eyes widened.

The waitress waved her hands back and forth. "Wait! We've got some hot dogs. I think they're made out of pork."

Said the human next to him, "I'll buy him an Awful-Awful."

"We have plant-milk ice cream."

"Ain't the same," said the human in disgust.

Fillio looked from one to the other. He knew that humans were omnivores and ate his kind, but what was an Awful-Awful? Whatever it was, it had to be bad to be doubly named.

"Hey, I got some tofu dogs back here," called the cook. "They're maybe a couple of years old. Freeze-dried, though."

Fillio shook his head. He got up. "Change your sign," he said, pointing to the golden cow on the green background. "False advertising."

His hooves hit the linoleum with a loud thump as he got off the stool. He sniffed, and his stomach roiled, smelling the greasy cooking meat.

He nearly ran out the door. After taking a few cleansing sniffs, he was better. He looked across the way to see a sign with a tree and fruit on it.

The sign of the golden cow was not a sign for bovines like himself, but what they served.

*Barbarians.*

✂

**Lisa Jacob** writes under the name L. A. Jacob. As Lisa Jacob, she writes contemporary fiction and romance novels. As L. A. Jacob, she

## L.A. Jacob

writes young/new adult urban fantasy, science fiction, and magical real-ism. Her most recent novel is a romance, *Carnival Farm*. She and her son are the servants of three feline overlords in Central Falls, Rhode Island. Email her at <u>warwriter@gmail.com</u>.

# McCoy

*by Barbara Ann Whitman*


The snow had barely melted,
a chill hung in the air;
The sounds and sights and smells -
nothing could compare!
Concrete cold beneath our feet,
the unyielding seats were cruel.
We bundled up against the wind
for springtime's favorite duel.

We warmed our hands with coffee,
cradling steaming Styrofoam.
The weather didn't matter
when the Pawsox played at home!
Behind home plate, just to the left,
best tickets at McCoy.
We waited long, through winter's dark,
to find this bit of joy.

Walking through the gates
with reverence and regard,
We'd gaze out toward the greenest grass,
in Ben Mondor's backyard.
In the air, you could feel
the ghosts of guts and grit
That every player ever toiled,
for that immortal hit.

In summer, there'd be fireworks
of red and gold and blue.
They filled the PawSox stadium
with an eerie smoky hue.

We'd snack on hotdogs, peanuts,
and an ice-cold foamy beer.
If they lost, we'd speculate
and say, "Maybe next year."

We'd ride our bikes when we were young,
when practice was beginning.
Then ride home in the dark,
when there were extra innings.
The boys would bring their gloves
and hope to catch foul balls.
Then cheer instead when their favorite player
hit one toward the wall.

Eventually we drove ourselves
in cars borrowed from our folks.
In later years, I took my kids,
sharing the memories it invoked.
My son, in high school, took the field
and played beloved McCoy.
My pride-filled heart swelled to watch:
My favorite all-star was my boy!

Another generation when
my grandson came along:
So much in life was changing,
but baseball still belonged.
When he was ten, we joined the Scouts'
opening ceremony on the infield.
Then, following the final out,
we pitched our tent in centerfield!

I loved the PawSox and McCoy,
for half a century or more.
I never dreamed that destiny
would one day close their doors.
I'm thankful for the memories

and countless days of pleasure.
In my life, McCoy Stadium
remains a precious treasure.

og

**Barbara Ann Whitman**'s writing falls across many genres, including her young adult/crossover novel, *Have Mercy*, about a young woman's journey from the foster care system to adulthood. Her work has also been published in all seven ARIA Anthologies, including a short story, a children's story, and poetry.

She has been a Sunday School teacher, Youth Group leader, a Big Sister, a parenting class instructor, and a Girl Scout leader. She has served on the board of directors at Big Sisters of RI, the Old Fiddlers Club of RI, St. Thomas Episcopal church in Greenville, and Gaits of Harmony, a therapeutic riding program. Her other interests include photography, antiques, camping, dancing, and the beach. She enjoys mentoring young writers, speaking to groups and she helps facilitate a writer's group at the local library.

# Christmas in Watch Hill

*by Debbie Howarth*

Counting down, "1,2,3,4,5,6,7,8,9, - 10!" Christine shrieked as she tore across the lawn. The summer sun was in her eyes, which made it hard for her to see where Matteo was hiding. Late afternoon was her favorite time to be outside. Her mother and sister would never come outside now; her mother said it would ruin their complexion, and often chided Christine for her tomboy ways.

"Christine Isabelle, it is 1929 and this is no way for a young lady to behave."

Father was back in the city working. He worked for Standard Oil, or rather a subsidiary of, and spent his week in New York City. Christine sighed. Matteo was her only friend at The Ocean House. This was her family's second summer at the resort in Watch Hill, Rhode Island, over-looking the Atlantic Ocean. She met Matteo last summer. Christine tiptoed behind the tennis courts about to scream "tag," but caught herself as she saw Matteo and his father, one of the groundskeepers.

"You have work to do, Matteo, you do not have time to spend on the guests!"

"Christine is my friend, Papa."

"You have no friends here, son. We work." Matteo's father Carmelo walked off in a gruff. Christine was sad. Matteo was only twelve. He should be able to play and not have to work all the time. Matteo waved goodbye and Christine waved back. No doubt her mother would be looking for her.

When Christine returned to the room she shared with her sister Claire, she pulled out her journal. Aside from her friendship with Matteo, writing in her journal was her favorite thing to do. Claire was sixteen and focused on her debut into society. She was not interested in Christine and her adventures. Christine started writing,

*"Everyone is talking about the golfer Walter Hagen who won the British Open in May. Matteo says he likes baseball better than golf. He told me that the staff plays baseball during their downtime. He loves the Summer Field Days, the one time during the season when guests and staff play baseball on the baseball diamond behind the hotel. He wants to play baseball and hit like Babe Ruth!"*

Yesterday Christine and her mother, Mrs. Armstrong, visited the small shops in the nearby town of Westerly. One of the shops had Christmas decorations. Christine was amazed at the intricate designs. "I wonder what Christmas at The Ocean House would be like. I bet it's magical!" The Ocean House closed each year after the summer season. Mrs. Armstrong went on to the pharmacy to pick up a preparation for her headaches. When she returned, she had a small medicine bottle that said Barbour's Pharmacy, Westerly, Rhode Island. What a pretty bottle, Christine thought to herself. It would make a nice vase for flowers. She looked forward to summers in Watch Hill all year and tried to bring back to the city as much of her trip as she could.

Emmy closed her grandmother Christine's journal. 1929 was certainly different from 2010, she thought dreamily. The slamming of a car door brought Emmy back to 2010. She ran to the window. Her smile faded as she saw her grandmother's caregiver Mary take her grandmother out in her wheelchair. Grandma was going to a nursing home. She was forgetful sometimes and mother worried about her staying home alone.

Emmy's mother, Margaret, tried to console her. "Grandma will have friends to talk to and people to take care of her all of the time." Emmy was sad, grandma was *her* best friend – she had someone to talk to here at *home*. Grandma didn't want Emmy to see her off; they had said their goodbyes at breakfast. Emmy consoled herself by reading Grandma's journals. Grandma had been reading the journals to Emmy since she was little, and now at 10 years old, they were still her favorite books to read. Emmy's favorite stories were of Grandma and her friend Matteo playing on the grounds of The Ocean House. Grandma's stories made the resort seem like a magical place. Emmy wanted to go there, but it had closed several years ago.

It had been a rough year for Emmy and her family. In addition to Grandma's move to the nursing home, Emmy's parents, Margaret and William, had separated. Emmy was heartbroken. Grandma was helping Emmy come to terms with it. Grandma would reassure Emmy, "I love you. Both of your parents love you. But it is up to your parents to manage this – and they will do what is best."

Emmy and her mother visited Grandma Christine every Sunday. It was harder and harder to say goodbye. One Sunday in early November, Grandma asked Emmy to go down the hall to see what was on the dinner menu. Emmy knew that Grandma wanted to talk to her mother and didn't want her to hear their conversation. When Emmy returned, they were finished, and Emmy's mother was getting ready to go. They said their goodbyes and left.

Two weeks later, Emmy was in her room reading grandma's journals when her mother came in. "Emmy, I was thinking about Christmas." Emmy's eyes lit up. Her mother continued, "The Ocean House in Rhode Island just reopened after its reconstruction. Grandma would like us to spend Christmas there."

"Really? The four of us will be going to The Ocean House?"

Emmy's mother bit her lip. "No, honey, just you and me. The travel would be too much for Grandma, and I am not sure of your father's plans, he may need to work. You'll see them both after Christmas."

"That's not fair! Grandma has always wanted to go back!" Emmy balled herself up in a pout.

"I know, Emmy. She wants us to go, that is her gift to you. I'm sorry, honey, it's the best I can do." Emmy's mother wiped away a tear, then got up and left.

After her mother left, Emmy picked up Grandma Christine's journals again. Grandma and her friend Matteo had a great time playing at The Ocean House. She always wanted to go back, but she never did. Grandma's father lost his job, and they lost their money in the Great Depression. Grandma never saw her friend Matteo again. The only thing Grandma had left were her journals. After hearing stories all of her life about Grandma Christine's adventures, Emmy was starting to look forward to spending Christmas with her mother at The Ocean House.

Mother and daughter arrived at The Ocean House two days before Christmas. "Mom, I want to make Christmas cookies."

"We can make them when we get home, Emmy. I am sure The Ocean House has many Christmas activities!"

The guest service representative tried to hide his excitement from his guests. "Mrs. Graham and Miss Graham, welcome to The Ocean House. We are so pleased that you will be staying with us over the holidays. My name is George. Please let us know how we may make your stay special."

"Thank you, George." Mrs. Graham smiled. She took Emmy's hand and followed the bellman to their room.

After the bellman left, there was a knock at the door.

"Good afternoon. Mrs. Graham. I am Jeanette, George's colleague. We heard that your daughter would like to make Christmas cookies. The pastry chef would like to invite you both to our kitchen this afternoon."

"I am a bit tired, but I believe Emmy would enjoy that very much. Emmy? You have been invited to make Christmas cookies."

"Really? I get to make Christmas cookies in *your* kitchen?" she asked Jeanette.

"Yes," Jeanette replied.

"Yes, I would like to go. Will you be okay, Mom?"

"Yes dear, I think I will take a nap until you get back."

"Any news on Dad?"

"I'm not sure he'll be coming, he has a room here, but the end of the year is a busy time for his firm."

Emmy sighed. Her parents' work kept them busy. Her father on Wall Street and her mother in advertising on Madison Avenue, but Emmy decided she was more excited to make Christmas cookies than dwell on her parents.

Emmy followed Jeanette down the hall past different rooms with lots of doors and halls. She wondered what mysteries and treasures they held. She arrived in the baking kitchen and was in awe of the cookies, cakes, and pies the bakers were creating. A large gingerbread house made the other desserts pale in comparison. The pastry chef, Grace, brought Emmy to a small table in the corner of the room. There was a bowl of cookie dough, a rolling pin and cookie cutters. Her assistant brought out a small apron.

"Let's get you ready to bake." She placed the small apron over Emmy's head and tied it around her waist. Chef Grace showed Emmy how to roll out the dough to the proper thickness. Emmy carefully chose the star as her first cutter, and Chef Grace helped Emmy press it into the firm dough. She then showed her how to move the cookie to the cookie sheet. Emmy then used the snowman and Santa Claus cutters. Emmy eventually used all of the cutters on the plate. The chef baked the cookies in the great oven.

Once the cookies were done, they were transferred to a rack to cool. She took Emmy to decorate the cookies. Emmy saw icings in several colors, silver and gold balls, sprinkles, colored sugars, and much more. Emmy started decorating, and Chef Grace was impressed with Emmy's talent.

"I love to decorate cookies," Emmy shared.

When Emmy was done, Chef Grace brought milk and cookies out so Emmy could have a snack while she waited for her cookies to dry. Emmy marveled at all that was going on around her.

"Emmy, I hope you enjoyed your afternoon," said Chef Grace as she handed Emmy the cookie tin filled with her Christmas cookies.

"Oh yes, thank you, Chef Grace!"

Jeanette took Emmy through the decorated lobby back to her room. Emmy imagined what other adventures she'd have while at The Ocean House.

The next day was Christmas Eve and Mrs. Graham arranged for Emmy to attend the children's activities, where they'd be making gifts.

"Mom, did you bring Grandma's journals with you?"

"Yes, just the ones where she talked about her visits to The Ocean House."

"What'd Matteo make that sounded like a Christmas ornament?"

"Well, let's see." Mrs. Graham retrieved the book. Having memorized them over the years, she knew which volume Emmy was thinking about. "Here it is. Mama wrote, 'Matteo and I walked along the beach after supper. The adults were busy in the dining room eating and enjoying the entertainment. We combed the beach for treasures. Matteo and I found bits of driftwood, sea glass, and seashells. We snuck into the crafts room to find paste and wire to make our creations. I made a bracelet with the wire, alternating pieces of sea glass and shell. Matteo took the oval sea glass and attached a small piece of shell that made it look like a bird. He attached the wire to the driftwood and then added the bird, to make it look like it was sitting on its perch. He found some paint and made the sea glass look like it had feathers. When he was done, he gave the bird to me, asking me to put it on my Christmas tree. I am so selfish! I should have made something for Matteo. Matteo said we should leave before someone finds us or Mother starts to worry. I was too embarrassed to look Matteo in the eye. I'll need to think of something to give him.'"

Emmy looked at her mother with a big smile. "That's what I'll do, I'll make a bird ornament like Matteo made for Grandma!" Emmy bounded off the sofa and tore down the hall to the elevator.

"No running, Emmy!" Mrs. Graham knew her remarks fell on deaf ears. She sat back on the sofa rereading her mother's words. Mrs. Graham smiled as she thought about the beautiful bird ornament that Matteo made for her mother. "I wish she was here," Margaret said with a sigh. She pulled out a wrapped gift and placed it on the nightstand near Emmy's bed. Margaret thought to herself, it is time Emmy started her own journal about her adventures at The Ocean House.

Jennifer, the children's activity coordinator, ushered the children into the workshop.

"Hi, I am Emmy, what is your name?"

"I'm David, nice to meet you."

"What are you making?"

"I want to make a boat. My granddad sails and I want to make a replica of our sailboat."

"Very cool. I want to make a bird ornament," Emmy stated.

Emmy and David walked over to the materials table. There were beads, sea glass, seashells, twigs, driftwood, ribbons, pinecones, acorns, birdseed, wire, cord, plus boxes and bags of other materials. Jennifer was there to help. Emmy explained the bird ornament to her.

"Emmy, how big should the ornament be?" Emmy put her hands together to form a ball. "That looks like about five to six inches in diameter. Why don't we start with the driftwood since that will determine its width?"

"Great idea." They found a piece of driftwood about ten inches long. Emmy chose the part she liked, and Jennifer cut it with a small saw. Emmy went to the sea glass and found a nice piece of glass to serve as the body. She then found a shell for the beak. She found the wire and a blue ribbon to match the sea glass.

"Emmy, is there anything else that you need?"

"Jennifer, do you have glue?"

"Yes, I have a glue gun that will work nicely." Jennifer brought over the hot glue gun to help Emmy put her ornament together. Emmy painted the feathers on the glass. As she waited for it to dry, she helped David hold the parts of his sailboat as he glued them together.

Everyone else had finished their crafts and left. Emmy wanted to be sure the paint on her ornament was good and dry, so she sat with David as he waited for the paint on his sailboat to dry. She then helped him to hang the sails. Jennifer brought a small box for Emmy's ornament and a larger box for David's sailboat. They sat and wrapped them together.

"Are you here with your family, Emmy?" David asked.

"Yes, I am here with my mother. Unfortunately, my grandma isn't here. She just went to a nursing home, and I will see her after Christmas. The bird ornament is for her. She used to take care of me."

"I'm sorry, Emmy."

"Thanks."

"I am here with my grandfather. He decided he wanted to be here, so we came early. The rest of the family will be joining us tonight. My grandmother died earlier this year. I miss her, and my grandfather isn't taking it well. The Ocean House is his favorite place, and he wanted to be here for the resort's first Christmas."

"I'm sorry about your grandmother. David," Emmy said consolingly.

As they were leaving the workshop, Emmy noticed some old wood in the back corner of the workshop. "What is that for?" she asked.

Jennifer replied, "The resort was closed while it was being rebuilt. They took the old hotel apart. numbering and labeling each piece. Then they rebuilt it, brought it up to today's building codes and included modern technology. However, we have some of the leftover wood and materials, so if we need to make repairs, we have pieces that will match."

Emmy stared at the wood pile. Something caught her eye. There was a piece of wood from an old fireplace mantle. It had paper stuck in a crack. After several strong tugs, Emmy pulled the paper out. She unfolded it and saw a list. Emmy slipped the paper in her pocket. Luckily, Jennifer wasn't paying attention because her co-worker had come to ask a question.

"Oh, it's lunchtime," Emmy said. David smiled and nodded. They both thanked Jennifer for her help and headed towards the dining room.

David and Emmy walked into the lobby past the large pebble fireplace. Emmy wondered how many Christmas stockings could be hung there. As David and Emmy waited their turn at the hostess stand, Emmy marveled at the three Christmas trees displayed on the side table. The trees were made of inverted seashells. She recognized the blue mussel shells – mussels were a favorite of her grandma. The upside-down mussel shells made the branches of the Christmas tree, and each shell held a pearl as its ornament. Emmy must have had a quizzical look on her face because David said, "Oysters."

"What?"

"Oysters, that tree is made from upside-down oyster shells." Emmy admired their pearl ornaments as well. It was now their turn in line.

"Hi, I am Emmy Graham. I am meeting my mother, Margaret Graham."

"Hi, Miss Graham, your mother said to order lunch and we can bring it to your suite."

"Hi, I am David Randolph, I am here to meet my grandfather."

"Yes, Mr. Randolph, please come this way."

"No, Miss Graham is my friend, and she'll be joining us."

"David, are you sure? Your grandfather won't mind if I join you?"

"No, he'd say it would be rude if I didn't invite you to eat with us."

David's grandfather stood up as they approached the table.

"Hi Grandad, this is my friend Emmy. Do you mind if she joins us?"

"No, of course not. Hello, Emmy, welcome."

"Hello, Mr. Randolph, it's nice to meet you."

"Actually, Emmy, I'm Mr. Triano. David's mother is my daughter." After they placed their lunch orders, Mr. Triano started the conversation. "So, Emmy, tell me about yourself."

"I'm ten and I'm here with my mother. My grandmother spent summers at The Ocean House when she was a little girl. She's in a nursing home and couldn't come with us, but her gift to us is Christmas at The Ocean House."

"And what about your father?"

"Dad needs to work so he's staying in the city." It was her patented answer whenever anyone asked about her father.

"Oh, what does he do?"

"He works for a venture capital firm."

"And your mother?"

"She's in advertising."

"Wonderful, I was in construction, and my late wife ran our family's philanthropic foundation. David's parents manage all of that now. I live with my other daughter and son-in-law in Boston." One of Mr. Triano's friends stopped by, and the conversation turned to drinks in the Club Room before the members' holiday party that evening. Mr. Triano seemed sad. He wasn't going for drinks or the party, no matter how much his friend encouraged him. Emmy could tell he missed Mrs. Triano.

"So, what did you find?" David asked.

"What do you mean?" Emmy replied.

"The paper you pulled out of that chunk of wood."

"It looks like a list, but I haven't really taken a look at it."

"We can do that after lunch," David offered. .

They entered the living room of her suite. Emmy pulled out the paper and spread it on the table. They sat on the sofa to examine it. At the top of the page it read, "C+M Treasures."

"Wow, a scavenger hunt, how fun!" Emmy exclaimed.

"That's cool," David replied, then asked, "What do we have to do?"

"We'll need to find everything on the list."

The page was creased, but only yellowed on the edges that were exposed to sunlight while in the mantle. The list had fifteen items.

*C+M Treasures*
*1. 3 different seashells*
*2. Sea glass*
*3. Driftwood*
*4. Something fuzzy*
*5. Something purple*
*6. A bird's feather*
*7. A spider's web*
*8. A soda bottle top*
*9. A playing card*
*10. Restaurant advertisement*
*11. A token from the old Shore Line Electric Railway*
*12. A souvenir from the Watch Hill Carousel*
*13. A horseshoe from the stable*
*14. A small glass bottle from a local store*
*15. A piece of pink granite*

"Some of the items we can find here at The Ocean House. Where'll we find the others?" Emmy asked.

"I think we can find the others in town. I can ask Grandfather to take us to Westerly. There are shops there. He'll know where to find them."

"That's a great idea, David, let's get started."

Emmy and David went to the front desk to ask for a small box to collect their treasures after leaving notes for Emmy's mom and David's grandfather. They headed to the beach to find the first three items, three different seashells, sea glass, and driftwood. David found a pretty blue piece of sea glass. "Emmy, this reminds me of the glass you used for your ornament."

"You're right, how pretty!"

There were mussel shells, clam shells, and a scallop shell, and some Emmy didn't recognize. Each went into their box. As they headed back towards the hotel, David found a small piece of driftwood sticking out of the sand. There was a dark grey bird's feather nearby. "Two more items for our collection!" David exclaimed. "What's next on the list, Emmy?"

The children ran to the workshop where they found the list. They literally ran into Jennifer, the activities coordinator. "Whoa, David and Emmy, where are you going in such a rush?"

"Hi, Jennifer! We're on a scavenger hunt. We need some help finding items," David announced.

"I see," Jennifer said. "What are you looking for?"

"Something fuzzy, something purple, and a playing card," Emmy explained.

"Well, let's see what we have." Jennifer brought Emmy and David to the craft table.

"Here are some cotton balls and purple ribbon." Jennifer gave them two of each and Emmy put them in the box. Jennifer went to the office and found a deck of cards.

"Here you go, it's better to give you the deck than just one card." She turned to David. "What's next on your list?"

"Do you have a stick?" David asked.

"Why, that isn't on the list?" Emmy said.

Jennifer handed David an ice cream stick, and David went to the window. He used the stick to carefully remove a small cobweb from the corner of the window. Jennifer took a small plastic bag from the craft table and held it open as David carefully placed the web and stick into it.

"One spider web!" Emmy said as she crossed it off of the list.

"What's next?" David asked.

"I don't know." Emmy stated. Jennifer looked over Emmy's shoulder at the list.

"Hmmm. I don't know if you'll be able to find the rest of your items here." Jennifer thought for a moment. "You should go to town. The shops in Westerly may have what you need."

"Thank you, Jennifer!" Emmy and David both gave Jennifer a hug as they left the workshop.

Emmy and David gave each other knowing glances, then headed back to the hotel and David's suite. There they found David's grandfather reading a book.

"Well, hello, you two. How's the hunt?" David's grandfather asked.

"We're doing really well," Emmy said as she brought the box over to Mr. Triano to see their treasures.

"Wow, you have quite a collection here," Mr. Triano said, admiring the different items. "I once knew a girl who had eyes as blue as that sea glass!"

"Grandma?" David asked.

"No, before Grandma. Grandma had chestnut eyes."

"We need some help with the rest of the list," Emmy said as she handed the list to Mr. Triano and continued. "Jennifer, the activities coordinator said we should go to Westerly to find the rest of the items."

Mr. Triano stared at the rest of the list. He seemed to get choked up. "I think Jennifer is correct."

"Would you take us, Granddad?" David asked.

"Well, let's ask Emmy's mother if it's okay and we can go."

Mr. Triano, David, and Emmy found Mrs. Graham finishing a phone call when they walked in.

"Hello, Mrs. Graham. I'm Matt Triano, and this is my grandson, David Randolph. Emmy and David have become friends today, and are working on a scavenger hunt. They would like to go to Westerly to look for some of the items on their list. Would it be okay for me to take them, and would you like to join us?"

"Mr. Triano, it's a pleasure to meet you and David. I'm familiar with Triano Construction and the Triano Foundation. I've some Christmas tasks still to do, but Emmy can go with you to Westerly."

"Grandpa, how will we get there?" David asked.

"The Ocean House has a car that we can use while we're here. I'll see if it's available."

Mr. Triano, David, and Emmy drove to Westerly. The trio went into every shop that might have an item on their list. In the last shop, Mr.

Triano saw an old-fashioned soda case. He reached in and pulled out a bottle of soda. He asked for three cups and paid for his purchases. Mr. Triano removed the top of the bottle with his keychain and handed the bottle top to David, who put it in the box. The trio sat down in one of the booths nearby to look at their list and their treasures. Mr. Triano picked up the piece of pink granite that the children had found in one of the earlier shops. A tear was just noticeable in the corner of his eye.

"My family came here from Italy. My father was a stonecutter who came to work in the granite quarries here in Westerly. They were famous for pink granite. When my mother died, Father quit granite and went to work at The Ocean House, on the grounds. I used to help him. I remember it like it was yesterday. I miss my parents."

David gave his grandfather a hug.

They had one item left on the list, the carousel souvenir.

"We have one more place to go," said Mr. Triano.

They drove to the Watch Hill Carousel. The carousel was closed but Mr. Triano handed David and Emmy each a gold ring. "I saw them in the last shop." Mr. Triano explained that the horses were suspended on chains, and it was the oldest carousel of its kind. "When I was little, before the '38 Hurricane, the carousel had chariots, too. Children would reach for the gold ring, but the brass ring was best, you would get a free ride with that one."

"That's so cool," David exclaimed. He and Emmy put their rings in the box. "We'll have to come back in the summer for a ride." Emmy nodded in agreement.

They headed back to The Ocean House. It was Christmas Eve, so they had to get ready for the evening's activities.

"There you are!" Mr. Triano said happily to two couples standing in the lobby.

"Merry Christmas, Dad," the women said in unison.

David said, "Emmy, my mom is on the left and my Aunt Anna is on the right. That's my dad and my Uncle Stephen next to him. I don't know the man they're talking to, though."

"That's *my* dad!" Emmy shrieked. "Dad!" Emmy ran to him.

"Merry Christmas, Emmy!"

"I wasn't sure you were coming," Emmy said.

"I know, sweetie, I'm sorry." Will hugged his daughter. "I brought you a present." Sitting on the sofa behind her father was Grandma Christine and Emmy's mom.

"Grandma!!!" Emmy gave her grandmother a big hug. "I'm so glad you're here." Emmy left to get David. "Grandma, this is my friend David Randolph, we had our own adventure here at The Ocean House, just like you and Matteo!" Just as Emmy said 'Matteo,' the room fell silent.

"My grandfather's name is Matteo," said David. David ran to his grandfather to bring him into the conversation. "This is my grandfather, Matteo Triano."

"Mr. Triano, this is my grandma, Christine Armstrong Taylor," said Emmy.

"Christine?"

"Matteo?"

They took each other's hands as Matteo sat down next to Christine.

"My father lost all of his money in the stock market crash after that summer, so we never returned. I always wondered what happened to you," Christine said.

"I was here in Watch Hill for a few more years. Then I joined the Civilian Conservation Corps and learned how to build things. I got into construction, married, and had my family. They all work in the family businesses now," Matteo explained. "The children found a scavenger hunt, C+M, did you make that?"

"They found it?" Christine said with disbelief. "I made that as a gift for you, for the ornament."

"We just finished the list," Emmy announced.

"Well, Emmy, I guess you had your own Ocean House adventure!" said Grandma Christine.

Margaret Graham put her arms around Emmy and David, guiding them away to give her mom and Matteo some privacy. Emmy looked up at her.

"Dad's here."

"Yes, he called yesterday. He missed us and knew that we were missing Grandma. So, he offered to bring her up here so we could spend

Christmas together. We met David's family when they arrived. We'll be going to dinner together shortly," Mrs. Graham explained.

Grandma was right, Emmy thought to herself. The Ocean House *is* a magical place at Christmas.

ભ

**Debbie Howarth** is a university professor and former interim assistant dean who resides in Plainville, Massachusetts. During her 12-year hotel career she held positions in operations, sales & marketing, and management. She then moved to higher education, where she has been teaching business and hotel management courses for over eighteen years. Debbie has been a subject matter expert for news and travel publications such as NYTimes.com, Philly.com, and NBC News Business Travel. "Christmas in Watch Hill" (2022) is her first ARIA publication. Debbie is thrilled to bring together her love of historical fiction and one of Rhode Island's iconic treasures.

# Favorite Neighbor

*by Belle A. DeCosta*

**R**hode Island, also known as "Little Rhody," is the biggest little state in the Union. Like most things small, it has a bigger-than-life personality. Miles of beaches and rocky coastline encase seaside towns, grand and small alike, much as a necklace bejewels a woman's neck. It's home to two historic carousels: The Flying Horse in Watch Hill, built in 1876, making it the oldest in the United States, and the Looff in Riverside, constructed in 1895.

I have a picture of my grandfather as a young boy, in a sailor suit, standing in front of the Looff Carousel when it was part of Crescent Park. He loved to recount stories of his and his cousin Tilly's adventures visiting the amusement park. I look forward to this summer when I can bring my grandson to ride the same merry-go-round his great-great-grandpa enjoyed.

Rhode Island also proudly claims coffee syrup (for milk), hot wieners, Del's frozen lemonade, and stuffies as its native cuisine. Unable to imagine life without these palatable pleasures, Rhode Islanders regularly send care packages to the unfortunate souls who have moved out of state. Yes, I said *coffee* syrup, not chocolate. A hot weenie is most definitely not a hot dog. Del's is far more than a common slushy. And while Cape Cod and the Islands offer quahogs, no one can stuff them like we do.

And let's not forget our unique way of giving directions. Rhode Islanders never use landmarks that are currently in place. "Take a left where the Almacs used to be, go down a ways until you get to the light at the corner where the old Kmart was, and take a right." Heaven help you if you're from out of state!

Each of these things could be a story all their own, but as near and dear to my heart as they are, none is my most cherished piece of Rhode Island.

A little background... I moved to Rhode Island eight years ago, after a divorce. I had lived right over the state line in Seekonk, Massachusetts, for over forty years and ran a business in East Providence, Rhode Island, for twenty-five years. It was hardly a move of epic proportions –

just under four miles. East Providence's housing market was more afford-
able, living on a single income. I was familiar with the city, and it had the
easy highway access I needed for my business. I bought a small fixer-upper ranch with two old maple trees perfectly spaced to hang a rope ham-
mock, and set about making the house my own. Well, fixer-upper might
be a bit of an understatement. It had, as they say, good bones, but boy did
it need a makeover! The outside was so overgrown you could barely see
the front and one side of the house. The previously mentioned trees had
large branches hanging precariously over the roof, and the backyard was
dirt, not a blade of grass in sight. The inside had potential but was tired —
okay, more like exhausted and straight out of the 1950s. Still, something
about it spoke to me. From the moment the realtor and I walked through
the door, I knew I was home. Armed with a vision and more determination
than know-how, I rolled up my sleeves and got to work.

I live in a neighborhood of three-foot fences, so my neighbors and
I got to know each other as we worked in our yards. I quickly discovered
they were all willing to raise a hand for more than just a wave. One lent
me a power washer, taught me how to use it, and insisted on picking up
my loam and mulch in his truck to save me the delivery fee. Chatting over
the fence with a retired neighbor, I lamented how there weren't enough
weekend hours to accomplish all I wanted to get done before winter. Two
days later, I arrived home from work to a newly painted back fence. The
morning after a nasty windstorm, I awoke early to the sound of chainsaws.
I looked out the window and saw broken branches strewn across my backyard and dangling dangerously from the trees. One neighbor was on a lad-
der cutting them down, while the other sawed them into a manageable size.
I threw on my jeans and ran out to help their wives, who were busy collecting and tying the wood into bundles. These people barely knew me!
When I continued to thank them profusely, one wife hugged me and said,
"That's what we do around here." The other winked and said, "Hey, free
wood for the fire pit." I've since enjoyed many evenings around that pit
and done a whole lot of thank-you cooking, baking, and beer-buying over
the years.

But, as much as we all look out for one another, everyone agrees
the consummate neighbor lived in the old red house at the top of the street.
The family's door was open to all; they were always friendly and could
help with anything needed. I never left the property empty-handed. A large

family, they had spread out over the years, with properties all over Rhode Island and parts of southeastern Massachusetts and Connecticut. But the smallest homestead, built in 1929, was our neighborhood's to boast. Benny's. A one-of-a-kind, no-other-store-like-it, Benny's. Akin to its home state, Benny's had a larger-than-life personality. I believe that comes from the ability to offer so much in a small space.

The largest Benny's I ever shopped in was still small compared to most stores. Think pebble versus a boulder and our neighbor a grain of sand in comparison. Oh, but the treasures they offered! Everything from hardware to toys, automotive, electronics, paint, housewares, electrical, and plumbing. Furthermore, Benny's provided many choices, not just a spattering of products to settle on. They also sold TV trays, desks, bikes, tires, reading glasses, and any battery you could possibly need. Seasonal? Spring brought everything you required for lawn care and gardening, including lawnmowers, kiddie pools, sprinklers, patio furniture, beach equipment, Adirondack chairs, grills, and marshmallows. Fall offered rakes, leaf bags, tarps, sealers, lawn football flags, Halloween costumes, candy, and decorations. Speaking of holidays, you could take care of all your Christmas needs at Benny's. Trees, lights, decorations for inside and out, tree skirts, wrapping paper, bows, cards, and gifts. Winter brought ice melt, scrapers, shovels, hats, hand warmers, mittens, and gloves. All in one easy-to-navigate space.

It's where I bought my grass seed, furnace filter, deck stain, wheelbarrow, toaster oven, gutter guards, and light timer. My hardware and garden tools, extension cords, mops, dog treats, beach chairs, doormats, nails, a fire pit, spray paint, cleaning products, and a garden hose. Also, Snickers bars, last-minute cards, foil baking pans, a travel hairdryer, sunscreen, storage bins, bottled water, and had keys made…well, you get the idea. Benny's had it all. Their slogan was, "If Benny's doesn't have it, you don't need it." Agreed. Undoubtedly their stockroom possessed the same magical properties as Santa's sack. How else could they offer so much in such a small space, neatly displayed? Plus, you never had to look for their signature red vest-wearing employees. They were always present, smiling, and willing to help. And it was all just a short walk up the street.

But alas, like so many other pieces of quaint Americana, its time came to an end in 2017, and like most Rhode Islanders, I was heartbroken.

The owners said when announcing the closing, "Times have changed, and it's difficult for family-run chains to survive." A sad and unfortunate truth.

So, now, with a nostalgic sigh, I grab my car keys instead of sneakers and head out to the big box store bullies to make three or four stops instead of one. I roam the cavernous aisles in the acre-sized abysses looking for what I need, or, if I'm feeling particularly optimistic, someone to help me. Usually, I leave unaided and sometimes empty-handed. But after an exasperating afternoon of errands, I head home and manage a smile as I put my blinker on and think, take a right at the corner where Benny's used to be. Time's forward march may change some things, but never all.

That reminds me; I need to find out when the Looff Carousel opens for the season...

ɔ

**Belle A. DeCosta**'s memoir, Echoes in the Mirror, was published in June 2020, and her piece, An Introduction, is featured in the 2020 ARIA Anthology, Hope. Her novel, Treading Water, published November 2021, was awarded Finalist for Best First Novel by Next Generations Indie Book Awards 2022.

Belle has had a lifetime of involvement in dance and choreography. She is the creator and director of Tap N Time, a seated tap and rhythm class designed for the elderly. Previously, she owned Belle's School of Dance for 25 years, and was founder and director of VERVE Dance Co.

When not traveling to nursing homes to share her program, she enjoys spending time with her grandson, being in nature, dining with friends, and, of course, writing.

Belle makes her home in East Providence, RI, and is a proud member of ARIA - Association of Rhode Island Authors.

Visit her at http://www.belledecosta.com

# It's on the House

*by Douglas Levine*

**"** my privilege to introduce our outgoing president, Dr. Cory Stefanek, for our 2002 meeting closing address..."

**●●●**

Dom Flores beamed as his boss ascended the stage. He was part of Stefanek's hospital team — nurses, techs, physicians — cheering with thousands at the convention. Stefanek was a royal in medicine, a superior in the crafts of clinical care, education, and research. Owner of the association's ambitious agenda to promote holistic patient care and overcome disparities. A leader back at the hospital who showed the house staff the ropes. An equal in the team who shared accomplishments. Everyone wanted to work with this doctor. Beneficence incarnate. Dom loved to support Stefanek and the crew's missions, be in the pit with this resolute squad, and teach and practice medicine.

Dom knew every word of the speech. Stefanek rehearsed it with the team, took suggestions, and revised it before the meeting. The hubbub in the hall continued and Dom's mind drifted. What drove him here?

The most important thing is your health. Dom's father's favorite saying. A bellwether. An alert for storms. Dom was eight when he lost a grandpa to pneumonia and a grandma to cancer. In middle school, a friend drowned in the river. Another got leukemia. Then his sister's accident. What could anyone do to help?

College was Dom's goal. But after? Aptitude tests showed he could be a religious leader or a medical doctor. Not a businessperson like his mom. Not a chemist like his dad. Not a race car driver. He was as uncertain about his future as the New England weather.

Dom's mother said, "Talk to Dr. Ricci." The family doctor and physician icon of the community.

Dr. Ricci finished Dom's pre-college check-up and asked about hobbies, grades, interests. "It takes more than ten years." Dr. Ricci whacked a stethoscope to sway like a pendulum. "After four in college, there's four in medical school, then three or more in a hospital residency. More after that for specialty training. Can't tell you what to do ..." Dr. Ricci knew Dom had applied to fifteen colleges and was accepted to only one. "...but Dom. You don't have to be a genius to get into med school." Dom wasn't sure what to be least confident about: his intellect, the results of his physical, or what Dr. Ricci prescribed for his hay fever.

In college, Dom earned grades needed for medical school. Dr. Ricci's advice led him to apply to thirty. Again, Dom was accepted to only one. He did not mind the work for the forms and interviews. One acceptance was enough.

"You got in, Dom." Dr. Ricci said. "I knew you could do it."

Medical school was like puzzle pieces. Where were the patients? Dom reported for Anatomy Lab and met his cadaver, the only whole person, more or less, he worked with for two years, aside from his instructors and classmates. There to dissect and learn the human being's parts, Dom welcomed the look under the hood, but he would not be ready to drive with a real patient for years. More puzzles awaited: structure and function of body parts, abnormalities in disease, bugs causing infections, drugs to treat disorders. Always a focus on parts with the same approach as Dom met patients on clinical services: He learned about hearts on Cardiology, lungs on Pulmonary, kidneys on Nephrology, minds on Psychiatry, intestines on Gastroenterology, bones and joints on Rheumatology, seizures on Neurology, rashes on Dermatology. A specialty for every part, Dom wondered how they fit together.

During his last year in med school, Dom applied for hospital residency slots at twenty different programs, the maximum number recommended. The match process abided by applicants' and programs' rank-order preferences. Although everyone could not get their top choices, a place was anticipated for every future resident. All parts came together. Dom celebrated with seniors across America on Match Day when they learned which hospital training programs they would enter. This time, Dom got his first pick. He had eyed it since he was a kid.

"Congratulations, Dom. That's a prestigious place," Dr. Ricci said.

In the 1950s, a younger Dom and his family often drove from the Boston area to Brooklyn to visit family. The seven-hour expeditions were meanderings on local roads before I-95 was completed. Dom wanted to drive the Plymouth before he could see over the steering wheel and reach the gas pedal. Denied this and his second choice to ride shotgun, Dom was consigned to the rear seat with his sister. There, they played I Spy as the world passed by through the side windows.

I Spy was better to play if there was something to see along the roads during nighttime journeys. The game was charged at both ends of the trip because of buildings aglow in Boston and New York. Between, there was New Haven, Bridgeport, Stamford, but not much else. Except for a city an hour from Boston. A welcome signal that home was but sixty minutes away on the return trip. Its name sounded like home. A future arrival. Fate. Destiny. Providence. Providence, Rhode Island. And near the future junction of I-95 and I-195 were the X-shaped wings of a prominent, ten-story structure, the one hospital Dom and his sister I Spied on their trips. X marked the spot for Dom's future training.

Dom's residency began in July 1979 at Rhode Island Hospital, one of the premier teaching hospitals affiliated with Brown University Medical School. Where newer construction now exists was a parking lot with spaces reserved for residents near the hospital's front entrance. Dom imagined a sign in the lot: "Welcome, you VIP, you!" After eight years around the racetrack in college and medical school, he was ready to save lives. The primo parking enlarged his sense of self-importance and entitlement as a new MD.

Dom recanted a bit whenever he approached his banged-up, two-door '73 Honda Civic. He could not ignore the dents, chips, and scratches, front headlight askew, droopy rear bumper, and bent radio antenna. To get in, he pried the driver's side door open with a crowbar that he kept in the hatchback's trunk. Before each trip to or from the hospital, he leaned into the ignition switch with his key for a half-minute-long resuscitative effort before the engine coughed, spewed out ominous, blue-black clouds of exhaust through the tailpipe, and sprang to life.

As it was for the other residents, Rhode Island Hospital was a house for Dom: He lived there with his wreck of a vehicle left idle in the lot. It took months of training during twenty-four- to thirty-six-hour shifts on ward, ER, and ICU rotations before he wised up. Before he understood what motivated the largesse of his coworkers. Before he appreciated the crudeness of the comparisons he made between the damaged parts of his jalopy and his patients' and the aptness of the analogies to his attitude. Dom first thought a parking spot so close to the hospital entry was a huge bonus. Each minute saved after he evacuated from or before he broke back into his car translated to an extra minute of sleep at his apartment. He came to understand that among the gifts he received while he trained at Rhode Island Hospital, sleep was one that could be overrated.

Dr. Dom Flores' re-education began on Day One and barely nicked his med school armor. Dynamism ruled: racing in fast-paced ward rounds run by staff physicians; scribbling clipboard notes to keep track; doing new patients' histories, physicals, and admission orders; endless recordkeeping; handing off orders for tests, prescriptions, and consults; beeping pager interruptions every two minutes signaling telephone extensions to call nurses or unit secretaries asking him to sign an order or confirm or debate one already written; finding bathrooms; getting overwhelmed by directions from consulting specialists; dodging technicians pushing x-ray equipment, EKG machines, IV poles, and gurneys with patients to mysterious places.

The day was a blur.

The day was like every day, a performance scripted, choreographed, and executed by ward nurses, nursing managers, unit secretaries, senior residents, and attending physicians. They ensured what needed to get done for patients got done.

Dom's roles were apprentice and scut puppy, an extra pair of hands, but he thought he was the lead player in a hospital that resembled the Seekonk Speedway. He recognized familiar puzzle parts from med school back when he had time to learn how they fit together. He was reluctant to apply the brakes on his confidence as hundreds of parts of multiple puzzles whizzed around in combinations that were tough to fathom.

Dom's first day was punctuated by what-do-I-do-nexts. When his hair was about to be set ablaze by a crash into overt panic, Britt — Dr. Brittney Bevilacqua — appeared to advise, and receded backstage until Dom's demeanor required her return. Britt was a second-year resident assigned to Dom to supervise and exert calm, his mooring in a maelstrom. She was a year ahead with the experience of three after working 120 hours per week during her first year. "It's like dog years," she said.

Day Two preceded Dom's first night on call. After another blurry day, he rushed to the cafeteria for a quick supper before returning to his patients. He fumbled with his wallet as he set his food tray down next to the cash register.

"Hello, Dr. Dominic Flores." The motherly monitor of the monies observed Dom's name tag and glanced at her notepad. "On call tonight, I see."

"Yes. Hi…Miss…Louisa," Dom reciprocated after reading her name embroidered on her uniform. Dom pulled out three bills. "Yes. First time—"

"No, hon." Louisa pushed his money back. "It's on the House."

"Really?"

"Yes, hon. Tomorrow's breakfast, too. All you can eat when you're on call. Come back for seconds. The hospital knows you work hard and need energy to take care of our patients."

Our patients? Dom thought. "Thank you."

The nurses, pharmacists, doctors — all patient care providers — of RIH (Rhode Island Hospital) were on a mission to stamp out disease like COPD (chronic obstructive pulmonary disease), CHF (congestive heart failure), and IBD (inflammatory bowel disease), among others, with especial attention to patient care quality and safety. To fulfill this mission as a teaching hospital, another malady unique to first-year medical residents — not nursing students or pharmacist interns — also had to be eliminated: EGO. EGO was not a medical acronym.

Diagnosis of EGO did not require a medical degree. It was identified by nurses, pharmacists, unit secretaries, technicians, security guards, custodians, cafeteria workers, candy stripers. Anyone with an RIH name tag. Patients and families. Senior residents, all of whom recovered from this affliction during their first year. Everyone who was not fresh out of med school wanted to rid the hospital of this mental miasma and occupational obstacle.

EGO was always cured at Rhode Island Hospital. The time course for resolution varied, subject to individual adjustments in the frequency of dishing out a curious elixir: treatment with Vitamin H. Vitamin H was not Hazing. Not the dispensing of the occasional "hon." Not Haloperidol prescribed for psychotic patients, although it was tempting to use on select residents. The formulation of Vitamin H varied according to each situation. It was administered to embed Humility and Help adopt a continuous learning mindset. Essential qualities for physicians to enable collaboration with nurses and other health care providers to properly care for patients. Dom received his share of treatment courses of Vitamin H.

The nursing manager of 10-A paged Dom. His patient, Mr. Deluca, had end-stage lung cancer and needed attention. Dom ran into the room, grateful that Mrs. Deluca was absent. He had befriended the couple and visited whenever he had a minute to spare. Mr. Deluca was unconscious and struggled to breathe. He looked terrible: His face was pale and his hands, arms, and legs were blue. His nurse reported the low oxygen and blood pressure levels and pointed to the slow heart rhythm on the cardiac monitor.

Britt observed from the hallway. She had advised Dom about options for patients whose demise was inevitable and who did not want aggressive measures to extend survival. "I'll bag him." Dom reached for a compressible Ambu-bag and face mask to hand-ventilate the lungs. An endotracheal tube and mechanical ventilator were prohibited because the patient was DNR (do not resuscitate). "Add dopamine for his blood pressure." Dom's puzzling about what to do next ended when Mr. Deluca stopped breathing and his heart rhythm went to flat line. Dom gently lifted his patient's hospital gown and placed his stethoscope on the chest to listen for heart or breath sounds. He lifted the device away and removed his earpieces, stunned by the immensity of the silence and questions that the field of medicine did not answer. Mr. Deluca was Dom's first patient to die.

"You did well," Britt said as she walked toward the nurses' station. "Let's do this right. Give me a few minutes so we're organized before we tell Mrs. Deluca."

Dom was upset and wanted to get this over with. Quickly. And he had five new patients on 10-A who needed admission work-ups and orders. Dom was not familiar with people's emotional responses when their loved ones passed. He was not aware of the custom for extended families to gather in Rhode Island Hospital's visitor lobbies to hold vigil as a matriarch or patriarch lay dying. But he chose not to wait for Britt and walked to the visitors' lobby. Inside, he saw Mrs. Deluca in the corner with two companions and shuffled toward them. Dom did not register Britt's code wailing from the hospital's intercom system: "PAGING DOCTOR SWOON. 10-A VISITOR LOBBY. REPEAT. PAGING DOCTOR SWOON. 10-A VISITOR LOBBY."

Dom's residency began before the COVID-19 pandemic, 9/11, and the bombing of the Alfred P. Murrah Federal Building in Oklahoma City. The HIV/AIDS epidemic lurked ahead. Unlike the working conditions for health care providers who managed through these and similar tragic situations, the circumstances at Rhode Island Hospital in 1979 usually allowed for dedicated focus on individual patients, uncomplicated by a need for emergent medical triage. But the facility was not immune to mass casualty events due, in part, to first-year medical residents.

Dom knelt before Mrs. Deluca to inform her of her husband's passing and reassured her that he died peacefully. She was calm, but the two people sitting with her raised hands to heads and shrieked. Dom's first clues that something other than his Civic's headlight was askew were the crashes of lobby furniture and thuds of bodies that hit the floor. He turned and saw chairs, floor lamps, and framed pictures on the walls toppled by flailing limbs. Visitors screamed and went down to the ground like dominoes. Two were prone in the middle of the room and convulsed. Dom entered a state of suspended animation as the catastrophe unfolded. Humans emulated expiring flies. Sixteen people must have suffered simultaneous, lethal heart attacks.

The nursing manager led the charge into the lobby followed by Britt. Her glare melted to a meld of grimace and smirk when she saw Dom's face. The cavalry soon arrived with nurses armed with smelling salts and residents toting blood pressure cuffs and IV poles with bags of saline. Two crash carts with cardiac monitors, resuscitation equipment, and medications were parked at the lobby entrance. Hospital staff initiated ministrations to the lobby's victims like a team well acquainted with this type of drill. Dom followed Britt's directions and was relieved to see Mr. Deluca's family members begin to revive and sit up with assistance. An hour later, Dom noted the final score: Fainting Spells, 16; Coronaries, 0.

"Same thing happened with my first," Britt said as she and Dom hoisted Mr. Deluca's sister into a wheelchair. "I'll never forget Mrs. Gomez. CHF. The body count was twenty-two."

"…and what you told me before I applied? I don't know if I'm cut out." Dom clenched the telephone receiver and paced around his apartment.

Dr. Ricci replied, "Dom. I was talking about getting into med school. I didn't say what happens after, except for how long it takes."

"I don't understand."

"You don't learn everything in med school. After, it takes genius to learn to know what you don't know. It's hard, but you figure out when to stop and ask yourself, 'What am I missing?' Then you find that stuff out. Everyone at the hospital wants to help. Hit the books, too, when you can."

"So, it's about experience?"

"Yes. That, but more. It's about doing what it takes. Being conscientious. Ha! Being conscious! Because you want to do your best for every patient. You'll do fine, Dom. I know. You're not afraid of demanding work. And you care about people."

"Thanks. That helps. I'll try to work harder—"

"Harder and smarter, Dom."

"Yes, Dr. Ricci. Um…where'd you say you did your residency?"

"I never told you? I trained at that same hospital of yours on Eddy Street."

One annoying form of EGO was rampant among first-year residents adulterated by a Y-chromosome and who thought that being called a male chauvinist was a commendation. Expression of male EGO commonly presented as arguments about some patient orders with the nurses, especially with those who were women. Nurses remained civil; they knew patients heard conversations in the halls and expected their doctors to be respected. But the nurses could seek a senior resident for help if they were being dissed. Dr. Tim Hardison was adept in the use of Vitamin H to address aberrant manifestations of testosterone.

Hardison was Chief Resident — an eminent, fourth-year role that preceded appointment to the medical school faculty — and a sheriff with authority to ride herd on unruly residents. Nurses, senior residents, and attendings respected him for his capabilities, collaboration, and instigation of team timeouts: Hardison worked with nurses to plan the first-year resident welcome picnic that featured burgers, Saugys, and softball. He cooked with nurses in a ward kitchen to do monthly johnnycake breakfasts for residents and nursing staff. He physically pulled residents whose shifts ended to Friday 18:00 Liver Rounds to join off-duty nurses and attendings to celebrate hospital teamwork with a 'Gansett or a glass of wine.

What was the source of Hardison's enthusiasm for gender equality? The influence of four older sisters in his formative years? The writings of Simone de Beauvoir, Betty Friedan, and Gloria Steinem? Hardison intimated it was his first-year resident butt getting kicked so often. "Hardison…" His senior resident rolled his eyes. "…you know zilch compared to the nurses. They've worked here for ten, twenty, or thirty years more than your four in med school. Do the math, Einstein." For Hardison, a form of genius amalgamated.

Hardison played one season with the Pawtucket Red Sox before he chose medical school over a career in baseball. He was a competitor. He hated to lose. He hated receiving Vitamin H as a first year resident but benefited. And, as Chief Resident, Hardison figured his rowdy, Y-chromosome-toting residents hated losing as much as he did as a minor leaguer and Rhode Island Hospital rookie resident. The 1973 battle of the sexes tennis match between Billie Jean King and Bobby Riggs was in the history books and was a milestone for women's rights. It provided the particular formulation for Hardison's prescriptions of Vitamin H to dispense.

"Flores!" Hardison overheard a "discussion" between Dom and a nurse. "Let her handle it. She knows what to do. And better than you. Come here."

"But—"

"Forget it. Say? Ever play squash?"

"No. I lettered in tennis in high school."

"I heard." Hardison mimed a tennis serve. "There's a squash court here. Way to let off steam. Lighter racket. Smaller ball. But no net. You play off the court floor and walls. I'll pair you up. Tuesday at 18:30 after you're done here." Hardison chuckled. "That's an order."

Dom met Hardison's accomplice, May Steensen, at the squash court. May had a master's in nursing and was a care provider and consultant to nurses on 10-A. Dom recalled "discussions" they had as he looked her over. Proficient at tennis, he knew he could take her in a squash match. Hardison concealed May's national titles and ranking in the sport. And her military service.

May explained the rules and they volleyed to warm up. When the game started, May transformed into a Nordic warrior goddess. She deceived Dom with drop shots and pelted the ball past him or ricocheted it at his head. THWACK. BONK! Dom piled up mileage with unproductive sprints and made more direct impact with the walls than the ball. THWACK. OOF! THWACK. CRUNCH! When May's winning rail and rebound shots went untouched by Dom's racket or other body parts, the cadence of the sound of the ball rocketing off her racket and bouncing into a corner was like that of Wagner's Ride of the Valkyries: THWACK-da-da-DUM-dum. THWACK-da-da-DUM-dum.

Sixty minutes elapsed and the 19:30 players showed up. "Nice match," May said. "Anytime you'd like to play again—"

"Right." Dom limped off the court on rubbery legs. He felt da-da-DUMB-dumb.

"Flores!" Hardison pulled Dom from the team on the next day's ward rounds. "Heard last night was a disaster." Dom was silent, unaware he was not May's first. Hardison knew that self-respecting first-year resident male chauvinists would not volunteer news to other self-respecting first-year resident male chauvinists about a drubbing on a squash court by a woman. Nor would a certain Valkyrie. The secret of Hardison's formulation of Vitamin H was secure for future use.

"You got beat by a girl?" Hardison's expression — part smile, part sneer, half of his upper lip curling towards a squinted eye — made "girl" sound like "geeeerl." Hardison directed the word down at Dom's head as if it would penetrate Dom's cranium and realign his Y-chromosome mental gears. Hardison saw a prominent lump centered above Dom's eyes. "Need an X-ray for that?"

Hardison, Britt, and Dom relaxed in the cafeteria before on-call duty that night. "Flores! The ward's under control. ER is quiet. Bevilacqua and I will cover. Sign out after supper and head to the dormitory. We'll page if things heat up." Before Dom objected, Hardison added, "Go. Take care of your head. That's an order." Britt smirked and stifled a giggle.

Dom plodded to the dorm through basement corridors that connected the hospital's buildings. What happened? Squashed on a squash court. Beaten by a geeeerl. Why were his relationships with nurses on the wards adversarial? Why did he treat them differently from Britt? Or did he? What about his mom? His sister? Other women—

"You look lost, Doc."

Dom turned toward the silhouette of a haloed figure holding a spear in his right hand. On closer inspection, he saw it was a broom handle.

"It's me, Doc. I helped you magically levitate that contraption on 10-A last week."

"Mr. Gabriel? Sorry. Couldn't see you."

"I'll replace the bulbs. So, as I said?"

"Took a wrong turn somewhere. Looking for the dorm."

"Didn't mean that kind of lost. Looks like you have ten sacks of potatoes on your shoulders."

"Um..."

"Looking for answers in that?" Gabriel pointed to the medical book Dom carried.

"Not sure."

"You know? When I'm that way, my missus gets my thoughts straight. Got a missus?"

"No, sir. Maybe someday."

"Well, you got a room key? You go that way to the end and you'll see the elevator."

"Thanks, Mr. Gabriel."

"Doc? Sometimes I got troubles I have to settle myself. After I sleep on them, most times I have the answers in the morning. Books can wait. No sin to catch some Zs."

What am I missing? Dr. Ricci's advice echoed in Dom's head the morning after when the throbbing from his skull bump subsided. What am I missing? Dom puzzled over the question before he left the dorm room for rounds. Then it hit him like a squash court wall: When it came to working with the nurses, he had to do much less telling and a lot more asking.

Dom asked and the nurses not only told but taught. Dom learned more about starting and securing IV lines and IV pump settings. When he asked about EKGs, the nurses showed him how to apply electrodes and remove them without yanking out chest hairs. He asked about what to prescribe for patients' anxiety and was enlightened about nursing approaches such as counseling, relaxation techniques, and massage therapy. Dom asked May to play squash regularly and he improved his game. May always won.

Laughter was good medicine for Dom when he realized he was not being laughed at and was being laughed with. He never knew when he was being set up — by Hardison, the nurses, the patients — but he never sustained body bruises from spoofs after that first squash match.

"How do we boost Mrs. Duran's nutrition?" Dom asked May.

"How about a coffee cabinet?" May transmitted a conspiratorial wink to Mrs. Duran.

Dom scratched his head. "Furniture comes in flavors?"

Mrs. Duran howled. "Oh, Doctor Flores. It's a drink. Ice cream, milk, and coffee syrup. Would you like one, too?"

Dom was assigned ER duty for one month. The rotation was ripe for spoofing because the staff knew the patients, but the patients were new to first-year residents. Like the pleasantly demented, elderly woman with recurrent asthma attacks who responded to inhalation treatments. When she was comfortable and able to speak, she asked Dom, "Want to hear a joke?"

"Sure, ma'am."

"Did you hear the one about the guy who lost his gal?"

"Don't think so."

"Well. He forgot where he laid her."

Dom's shock evaporated when he heard the staff behind him applaud and laugh. First-year residents who cared for "new" patients in the ER constituted a spectator sport:

A shackled repeat ER offender from the Cranston Adult Correctional Institution wanted fresh air and came in with complaints of "foaming." Every time he talked, bubbles were extruded from his mouth and nostrils. It took Dom twenty minutes to determine that he swallowed hair shampoo. Again.

Another regular lived on the streets and feared for his life only during electrical storms. Dom did not know the patient — the staff called him Mr. Chick Little — was allowed to stay in a room and sit under a stretcher in the dark until the sky stopped falling. Dom was confused about why he was required to sit cross-legged on the floor, interview and examine Mr. Little in the shadows, and jot notes using a penlight held between his teeth. Until the giggling percolated throughout the ER.

Dom recited the posted "ER case of the month" to the staff. "Listen to this one. 'PW, 34-year-old male from Woonsocket, thinks he has rabies. Found his woodchuck — he sleeps with it every night — unresponsive and not breathing in bed and performed CPR with mouth respirations without success. PW concerned about woodchuck's cause of death. Physical exam (of PW) normal. Blood drawn for general labs. Infectious Disease, Animal Control, Psychiatry consults ordered.'"

Dom asked about the patient's outcome. "Pending," an ER nurse said. Sleep-deprived, Dom had to be directed to the signature on the report: "Bea Bananas, MD," the pseudonym of a budding medical fiction writer, Dr. Brittney Bevilacqua …

"…and thank you, Dr. Stefanek. Let's give her another round of applause while her husband, Blake, and their family join for the presentation of the Association's President Medal to Cory…"

Dom applauded. Twenty years ago, he accepted Stefanek's job offer after he completed his three-year medical residency. Dom contacted his former Chief Resident that day in 1982 to share the news that she invited him to work with her at Rhode Island Hospital. "You got hired by a girl?" Hardison's incredulity was ironic in both principle and fact. Hardison and his and Dom's future wives already worked under Stefanek's direction. One year after Dom became his coworker, Hardison agreed to be Dom's best man contingent on first obliging May's request: to walk her down the aisle and deliver her to the church dais. Dom returned the honors when Britt and Hardison tied the knot the following year.

One week after the Association's 2002 celebration of Stefanek's presidential term, May, Britt, Hardison, and Dom ate lunch in the hospital cafeteria and discussed the agenda for their meeting at 13:00. Satisfied with the plan, they bantered for a few minutes. Dom and Hardison debated which of their fantasy sports, NASCAR and MLB, was imbued with more machismo. Hardison opined about the impact on these sports as women entered the ranks. Dom cringed whenever he heard the word "impact."

Britt looked up from her notes. "Do you two even know what 'machismo' means? And how come you never mention squash?"

May said, "You know, balls to the wall!"

"Ouch!" Hardison groaned, head in hands. "Flores! That's what I'm saying. Man, we're doomed."

"I hope our Captain May is referring to that." Dom pointed to the commotion in the food service area. "Here we go again." The boisterous band of first-year residents of 2002 lined up for lunch before their orientation meeting with the most experienced quartet of clinical educators in the hospital.

It was on May, Britt, Hardison, Dom, Stefanek, and every nurse, unit secretary, senior resident, attending — like Dr. Ricci — technician, security guard, custodian, and cafeteria worker to carry out Rhode Island Hospital's missions: Stamp out disease. Stamp out EGO. Care for patients. Ensure safe, quality care. Dispatch medical, nurse, and pharmacist trainees everywhere in the world to do the same.

And it was on everyone in the House to keep an infusion of hope, spirit, and humor flowing freely. Miss Louisa said it best at her cash register in 1979: "It's on the House."

# Douglas Levine

ଔ

**Douglas S. Levine**, a three-year member of the Association of Rhode Island Authors, had his first short story published in *Hope*, the ARIA Anthology of 2020. Doug is a physician scientist who works part-time as a consultant in the life sciences sector; his professional publications include medical articles in peer-reviewed journals and book chapters dating back to 1976. The platform for his belated efforts in fiction writing is his forty-plus years in health care doing clinical research, developing new diagnostics and treatments, providing medical care, and acquiring insights into patients' illness experiences. He resides in Seekonk, Massachusetts with his wife; they met in 1979 when they both worked at the iconic hospital that inspired "It's on the House." Doug is proud to have completed his medical residency training at Rhode Island Hospital between 1979 and 1982; it was an experience that set the direction and trajectory for a very happy personal life and a very satisfying professional career. Doug writes fiction under the pseudonym, Abraham Simon.

# Oscar

*by Deborah L. Halliday*

The sun streamed in, or night-time streetlights shone,
In every room a changing paradigm
Of lives misplaced, and memories windblown,
For here it was life's twilight all the time.
The squeaking med cart rattled down the hall
And loved ones laughed, or cried, or held a hand,
It all was done with loving protocol,
Providing comfort for mind's shifting sand.
With pitter-pats he roamed the halls and checked
To learn which person needed him that day;
Unfailingly his instincts were correct;
They knew the time approached with Oscar's stay.
Where death was coming Oscar could be found;
Insistent, he would never be deterred;
He leapt upon a bed in one soft bound,
Pressed closely to their side 'til afterward.
A sentinel perhaps, for spirits flown,
With Oscar there, none ever died alone.

ରେ

 Oscar the Therapy Cat lived his entire life in the dementia unit of the Steere House Nursing and Rehabilitation Center in Providence, Rhode Island. Very early in his life the staff noticed that Oscar, normally a bit standoffish, would always gravitate to patients in their last few hours of life. He seemed to know, sometimes before the staff did, who would die next. He would jump on their beds, curl up next to them, and stay until they died and the body was removed. He could get quite agitated if kept away. Staff and families both came to appreciate the comfort Oscar provided. In his seventeen years he accurately predicted and was present at well over 100 deaths. Oscar was the subject of a write-up in the Providence Journal, *an article in the* New England Journal of Medicine *(2007), and a book,* Making Rounds with Oscar *by David Dosa, M.D. (2010). Oscar died on Tuesday, February 22, 2022, a special palindromic day befitting this special and extraordinary cat.*

**Deborah L. Halliday** is living her life of retirement in Pawtuxet Village. To challenge herself with something new in her 60s she decided to try to write poetry, and as a born structural thinker she gravitated to the discipline of the sonnet. "Oscar" has too many lines to be a sonnet, but reflects the basic construction of that form. Deb is currently working on several sonnet collections which (someday) will be published under the umbrella title "Very Short Stories" since her poems are usually narratives based on historical people or events. She is thrilled to be able to help spread and immortalize awareness of Oscar's work and gift.

# Where Piccolo Mondo Caffè Used to Be

*by Alfred R. Crudale*

The warm August afternoon was resplendent with sun as I entered Tony's Colonial Market on Atwells Avenue. The aroma of imported Italian hams, salamis, and cheeses filled my senses as my eyes adjusted to the artificial light inside the store.

I entered the farthest aisle and walked to the end where the blue and white boxes of imported croissants filled with Nutella are stacked. The boys love it when I bring them home as it reminds them of their breakfasts in Italy. I then rounded the corner to the next aisle with its rows of Bialetti espresso pots and stacks of coffees from Italy. As I eased a can of Kimbo espresso from the shelf I noticed a handsome young man eyeing the array of coffees. He glanced over to me and asked, "Do you always drink that brand?"

"Whenever I can get it," I answered.

"I usually drink Medaglia d'Oro," he said.

"Oh no, not Medaglia d'Oro," I replied. "Kimbo is much better coffee. It is the most popular coffee in Napoli," I informed him.

"Okay, I'll try it. Thanks."

And with that I made my way over to the meat case where I purchased a stick of Tony's store-made hot Soppressata and a wedge of imported provolone.

After Gina, Tony's wife and co-owner of the market, rang up my acquisitions, I bid her and Tony *buona giornata*, then stepped into the sundrenched street. To my surprise, the young man from the coffee aisle was just outside the door.

"Hello again," I offered.

"Hi."

The sunlight afforded me a better look at him. He was quite dashing. Slim and just a bit taller than me, his dark hair was combed back off his forehead, and his brown eyes were kind and welcoming. His mustache, full but neatly trimmed, complemented his soft features. He looked very familiar. I seemed to think that I knew him, but I was not sure how.

"I'm going to Venda for a coffee, would you like to join me?" he asked.

Rather taken by his attention, I accepted his offer, and we walked the one block from Tony's to Venda Ravioli.

Once inside, we made our way to the rear of the store, past the large case of prepared foods and the refrigerator stacked with many types of fresh ravioli, and sat down at a small round metallic table just in front of the espresso bar. I ordered a double espresso and he, a cappuccino and a cannoli.

"Everything is so different," he began. "What happened to Piccolo Mondo?"

"Piccolo Mondo?" I questioned. "That hasn't been there in years. It's now Roma Foods."

"Yeah, I saw that. And what about Providence Cheese? I can't find Providence Cheese."

My eyes grew wide. "How long has it been since you've been on Federal Hill, my friend?"

Without answering my question he offered, "Well, at least Angelo's and the Old Canteen are still here."

"Yes. They're Rhode Island institutions, and let's hope they will remain so for many years to come."

"And what happened to St. John's Church?"

His question filled me with cautious awe. This man looked to be in his late teens or early twenties. It would be impossible that he could remember St. John's, which was demolished in the mid-1990s. I grew somewhat suspicious.

"How old are you?" I inquired.

"I'm twenty," he said.

"Then you cannot possibly remember St. John's Church, or Providence Cheese, or Piccolo Mondo, for that matter."

"I most certainly do. They were all here the last time I was on Federal Hill."

I was totally befuddled.

After paying for our coffees, I invited him to accompany me on a walk down Atwells Avenue. He enthusiastically agreed. We exited Venda onto DePasquale Square, crossed at the traffic light, and turned right. As we strolled the red brick sidewalk with the ornate black lamp posts, some adorned with the Italian colors, we passed Roma Foods. In front, at a small round table made of mother of pearl, sat three elderly men speaking Italian and sipping *limoncello* from petite crystal glasses. Another man at a separate table sat scrolling through his iPhone. My young friend stopped and stared at him. Turning back to me as we resumed our walk he asked, "What is that guy doing?"

"I don't know. Scrolling through his phone, I guess," I replied.

"His phone? What phone?"

"His iPhone," I replied.

Although he seemed totally perplexed, he dropped the subject.

The traffic was thick that afternoon. From a car with its windows open came extremely loud Hispanic music. Service trucks, delivery vans, and a Providence police cruiser all passed us headed in the opposite direction while we walked toward Holy Ghost Church. As we walked, an attractive lady wearing an elegant charcoal gray business suit passed us. My friend commented, "She's hot, but she's talking to herself."

"Nooo!" I informed him. "She was wearing earbuds."

"Earbuds?" he asked, but inquired no further.

I continued to interview him.

"So where are you from?" I began.

"I'm from Knightsville, in Cranston."

"Well, that's interesting," I replied. "I grew up in Knightsville many years ago."

"Wow, really?"

"Yes. Where in Knightsville do you live?"

"Well, we used to live on B Street. My grandparents have a two-story home and my two brothers, my parents, and I used to live in the apartment on the second floor."

His answer caused me to stop abruptly. I was very unsettled. As I stared at this young handsome stranger, I began to think he was a conman who was either mocking me or taking me for a fool. Fortunately, we had arrived at St. John's Park, and I suggested that we sit on one of the park benches.

"This is Saint John's Park, where the church used to be," I informed him.

"Yes, I saw it earlier. It's so weird."

"You said you used to live on B Street. Where do you live now?"

"About ten years ago my parents bought a house on Plaza Street, and we moved there."

With this answer the palms of my hands began to sweat and I felt nauseous. I took a deep breath to center myself. He noticed my behavior and gave me an inquisitive look. "Are you okay?" he asked.

"I'm fine," I replied. "Probably too much caffeine. I should not have had a double. Hey, we haven't introduced ourselves. I'm Al." I intentionally did not offer my last name.

"Wow, my name is Alfred, but all my friends call me Al." With this he offered me his hand, and with great reservation I shook it.

"So Al, may I call you Al?" I asked.

"Yeah, of course."

"So, Al, do you work?"

"Well, I work part-time at a store in Garden City called James Kaplan Jewelers, but I'm a full-time student at Rhode Island College. Are you sure you're okay? You're really pale."

I swallowed hard and replied, "I'll be fine. What are you studying at RIC?"

"I'm an education major. I'd like to teach Italian and Spanish at a high school."

"Interesting. I taught in Warwick for thirty years. Now that I'm retired I teach at URI."

"Really? What do you teach?"

"I teach Italian."

"Seriously? That's amazing."

"It most certainly is, my friend."

"I really want to teach Italian. I love Italy and I love speaking Italian."

"Yes, I know. And I bet you're very passionate about it."

"I am, but how would you know?

I dismissed his question. I needed to continue to control the conversation for I still was unsure of his game.

"So what year will you graduate?"

"1985," was his reply.

I nodded and asked, "What year is it?" This question was a mistake. He squinted and gave me a very curious look. I had aroused his suspicion, although that was not my intention. I needed to keep the conversation flowing.

"What year do you think it is?" he asked.

Not wanting to divulge the current year, I intentionally hesitated, which caused him obvious concern.

"I need to go."

As he rose from the bench, I gently placed my hand on his arm, saying, "No, no. Please stay. I want to talk to you about my experiences teaching Italian at the high school level." This seemed to calm him and he slowly sat back down. I recounted my stories about teaching at Toll Gate and Warwick Veterans High Schools. I told him about my experiences as a class advisor and coaching the Toll Gate soccer team. We discussed several activities I used in teaching my students Italian or Spanish grammar and vocabulary, and I explained how I had created two exchange programs; one with a high school in Seville, Spain and another with an Italian high school in the town of Alatri. During the conversation, he was very engaged and often laughed and asked me questions. At one point we became silent, and I noticed that the street was almost deserted except for an occasional passing vehicle. I decided to use the moment to rip open the situation.

"How would you respond if I told you it is the year 2022?" I began.

Once again his eyes narrowed, but he remained silent as he glared at me. I continued.

"And what would you say if I told you that I am your older self?"

He let out a raucous hysterical laugh. "That's absolutely ridiculous. You are a weird old man."

I was hurt that he saw me as an old man. While I realize that I am not young, at fifty-nine I do not consider myself old. In retrospect, however, speaking to my twenty-year-old self, I understood his perspective.

"No, think about it, Alfred. I also grew up in Knightsville. I also lived on Plaza Street. I also worked at Kaplan Jewelers. Do you see? You are me, thirty-nine years earlier."

"That's bull!" he responded. "I told you all that stuff."

"Yes, you did," I replied, "but you did not tell me that your grandfather on B Street owned a white Cadillac Deville, and you did not tell me that your maternal grandparents lived in a yellow house on Ashton Street in Providence, and you did not tell me that in high school you worked at Burger King on Fountain Street in downtown Providence."

His eyes were like saucers as he jettisoned himself from the park bench and turned to face me.

"How do you know all that? Who are you?"

"I'm Alfred Robert Crudale, and I was born on August 15, 1963. I live in South Kingstown on a small farm with my wife. I am a retired high school teacher and I teach Italian at the University of Rhode Island. Our brothers Anthony and Michael still live in

Cranston with their own families. Our dad has passed away, but our mom still lives in the big white house on Plaza Street."

"This is all too weird!" he said. "I'm leaving."

"No! Alfred, wait! Think about it. How could I possibly know so much about your past? Think about the man with the iPhone and the lady with the earbuds. Where is Saint John's Church? What has happened to Piccolo Mondo Caffè? Why can't you find Providence Cheese? These landmarks haven't existed for many years."

As his eyes shifted back and forth I knew his mind was racing. He desperately searched for a logical answer but was unable to find one. He stood before me very puzzled and visibly upset.

In a strong but calm voice I asked, "Are you still dating Lisa?"

"Yes!" he said abrasively. "And we're going to be married."

So not to upset him further, I hung my head and chuckled, but I could not bring myself to make eye contact with him. Slowly I lifted my head.

"No, you won't, actually. You will meet a beautiful woman who will complete your life and make you very happy. Would you like to know her name?"

"No!" he shouted. "You're a freaky old man! I should have never spoken to you in the market!"

"You and Barbara," I continued, "will have a lovely life together. You will have four wonderful sons of whom you will be extremely proud."

"Screw you, old man!"

"Alfred, do not fear your future. You have a very happy and rewarding life ahead of you."

He made a fist, and raising his middle finger thrust it toward my face. Then, turning, he sprinted up Atwells Avenue toward the place where Piccolo Mondo Caffè used to be.

I watched him disappear into the distance. I sat very quietly contemplating the afternoon's events. I felt great empathy for him as I imagine it must be very frightening to look forty years into the future and see a world which you no longer recognize, or to find that age and time have changed your physical beauty, as well as the plans and dreams you hold so dear. Placing my hands on my knees, I lifted myself off the park bench in front of where St. John's Church used to be. I crossed Atwells Avenue and turned to my right, walking toward Tony's Colonial Market and into the now setting sun.

ଓଷ

**Alfred R. Crudale** is a native Rhode Islander who grew up in the Knightsville section of Cranston. He has been an educator in Rhode Island for over thirty years and earned his Ph.D. in Italian literature from the University of Connecticut. He is a lecturer in the Italian department at the University of Rhode Island. He and his wife Barbara, the parents of four boys, live on their small farm in West Kingston, Rhode Island. In 2021 Bordighera Press published Crudale's book *The Voices of Italy: Italian Language Newspapers and Radio Programs in Rhode Island.*

# Green Stamp Summer

*by Rick Billings*

It was the summer that Grandma fell on the escalator at the Shepard store downcity. It was the summer that Grampa left his false teeth on a bench at Blackstone Boulevard. It was the summer of the great bike adventure to Lincoln Woods. It was the summer that we started noticing girls and good music. It was the summer of the PPMF and Jimmy Kelly. And it was the summer of my radio and the S&H Green Stamps.

My two best friends were Mickey and John. We'd been together for several years and many summers by then. In that way that only seems to happen with kids, we were all a little hazy on how we even met each other. I grew up living across the street from Payne Park on the somewhat darker side of Pawtucket. It was a big community playground in those days with a full summer recreational staff and a beautiful pool that seemed to have a thousand kids in it every time it was open. There was always a lot going on and it became our hub for the start of the day. If we were up early enough we would go out and search the playground for empty soda bottles left from the night before. Payne Park had a very different side after ten o'clock when the big lights went out. There was always ample evidence of the previous night's activity each morning. If we found enough bottles we would bring them to Conners Variety Store on West Avenue to cash them in and then split our haul. There would usually be an argument over which one of us was going to go into the store and face old Mrs. Conners. At some point during the transaction she would inevitably look you in the eye and say "I don't think all these bottles came from *this* store." She would then begrudgingly hand over the cash and whoever drew the short straw that day would skulk out of the store feeling like they'd stolen her life savings.

Our neighborhood, like most in those times, had a unique personality. The community was primarily Irish Catholic. Not all of the families interacted but most knew each other. Everyone went to St. Mary's Church on Sunday. The good majority of us kids went to St. Mary's School. Everyone shopped at the same stores, ate at the same pizza place, drank at the local bar, and when someone died went to the same funeral home, V.J. McAloon, right on the corner of Payne Park and West Avenue.

Almost every family had three or four kids. The moms went off in the morning to at least one part-time job while the dads worked at Moore Fabrics, Union Wadding, or Narragansett Wire. Throughout those summer days, untethered by school, we kids were on our own.

I was the youngest in the family and the only boy. The distance in years between my sisters and me made it necessary for me to stay with my grandparents a lot when I was younger. My mother would pick me up after work every day on her way home. Thursday was always my favorite because Thursday was grocery shopping day. After picking me up, we would drive by the Bean Hill Bar and pick up Dad's pay. In what seemed like a bizarre sort of parade, the moms would drive up in front of the bar, honk the horn, and the dad that identified with that particular car would put down his 'Gansett, run out, and hand over a portion of his earnings for the week. Sometimes we would see some of the same cars parked at the Almacs, the same moms shopping in the aisles.

I wish I could say that shopping day was my favorite because I enjoyed the quality time with my mother so much. My real motivation when I was little was that I might score a Matchbox car if I could get her to go down the toy aisle. As I got older the motivation changed a bit. I continued to go with her out of habit but so often with kids there's an ulterior motive. Enter the S&H Green Stamp.

In the early days of my market trips, Almacs was a bustling, fully staffed store. Every register had a cashier and a bag boy. After taking my mom's payment, the cashier would hand her the sales slip and a strip of S&H Green Stamps that corresponded to the amount that she spent. The bag boy would place the sacks of groceries into a gray metal bin. The bin had two yellow metal tags with a number. Mom would get one of the tags and the other remained on the bin as the boy loaded it onto a set of rollers that went across the front of the store and curved around to the outside. After getting the car, we would drive up and give the outside attendant our number and he would load the bags into the trunk. Every week, I asked my mother if I could ride in one of the bins to the outside. Every week she would answer with a quiet "no." It was the same tone of "no" that kids of that age hear every time they ask to do something that they know they can't do. I heard that "no" whenever we went to the Ann & Hope in Cumberland, too. After having my obligatory hot dog with celery salt and grape soda, I always asked her if I could ride in the shopping cart when it went down the medieval conveyor that brought the carts from the upper floor to the lower and back. It was obviously out of the question. "No."

It seemed that things changed at the Almacs very quickly. The New York Lace Store that was nestled next to the market closed, as did the Coats Field farther up Lonsdale Avenue. The numbers of cashiers and bag boys dwindled. The gray bins vanished and the rollers sat unused as shoppers became responsible for bringing their own groceries to the car. They still gave out Green Stamps, though. The store had installed a bright green S&H box above the registers. There were black dials on it similar to those on a rotary phone. After the transaction, the cashier would simply dial up the amount spent and the stamps would be dispensed.

The S&H Green Stamp store was on Pawtucket Avenue, close to my grandparents' house. They had a big catalog that seemed to have everything you could ever want. After the description of each item would be a statement in bold print that said how many books of stamps you'd need to redeem to get the item. It was all very simple and straightforward aside from the fact that someone had to do all the licking to get the stamps into the books.

Back in the spring I had been looking through the S&H catalog and noticed a transistor radio in the electronics section. Money was less than scarce in our household and a luxury like a personal radio was something that was only a possibility on birthdays and Christmas. As those were both a long way off, I grew obsessed with getting the S&H radio. I waited for an opportune moment to approach my mom about it. I was a quiet kid in a house that was often in turmoil and the perfect window for that kind of discussion was evasive. At that age, I was oblivious of her juggling three daughters, a son, and two aging parents without full participation from my dad.

The first time I got up the nerve to ask her, the phone rang as soon as I said "Mom?" She answered the phone and sighed. Her shoulders dropped just a bit as she said that she'd be there in just a few minutes.

"I have to go and get my mother," she said. "She fell on the escalator at Shepard's and banged up her knee." With that, she was gone.

The next time I figured I would ask as soon as she came home from work. My plan was dashed yet again by the grandparent factor. I heard her car pull up and waited by the door. She came in briskly and right away I could see that she had "The Look." I can only describe that look as a combination of annoyance, frustration, and a drop of anger atop the weariness that was the underlying feature so often on her face. None of us ever wanted to be the recipient of "The Look."

"I have to go back out. Your grandfather left his false teeth on a bench at the Boulevard and some kids decided that it might be fun to run over them with their bikes."

"But Mom," I said without thinking, "why did he take his teeth out at the Boulevard?"

She stopped and took one of those big, deep, mom breaths. Those are the miracle breaths that come from somewhere deep inside and prevent moms from screaming at the only person in the room because after all, he wasn't the one who left his teeth on a bench, or for that matter ran them over with his bike.

So in an impressive show of motherly restraint she said in a very low controlled voice, "I. Do. Not. Know. Why. He. Took. His. Teeth. Out." And with that, she was gone.

When all was said and done, the eventual conversation was very anticlimactic. All of the imagined arguments and reasonings never happened. She simply said that if I was willing to lick all of the stamps and put them in the books, then I could use them to get whatever I wanted. I'm not sure that she was aware of the bow-and-arrow set and the pellet gun that were also in the S&H catalog. Fortunately, I had my heart set on the radio.

The next three weeks found me licking and pasting little green stamps into little white books. I tried several methods of moistening them, but physically licking the stamps seemed to be the only thing that kept them in place. I could only stand to do it for a limited time. The resulting icky glue taste, green tongue and fingers put me off after I'd done a few pages. One-cent stamps were the worst, as it took fifty of them to fill a page. The tens were great to come by. Once in a while I scored a fifty-value stamp from the pile. The kitchen drawer that Mom kept the stamps in was overflowing. I was confident that I would have enough stamps for the radio. As it turned out, I was a little over one book shy.

I spent the next week in the kind of obsessive desperation that only a kid can have when he or she has fixated on something. I walked down to Almacs and checked the parking lot and around back. I asked Mickey and John's moms for their stamps and pestered my grandmother and Aunt Murie. I tried to muster the courage to ask shoppers leaving Almacs if I could have their stamps but I chickened out. In what I thought was a brilliant and devious move I even padded the grocery list so that if Mom spent more money I would get more stamps. Within a week or two, I somehow mustered up enough stamps to fill the books that I needed.

Early one morning, I met Mickey and John at the halfway point between our houses and we walked up to the S&H Green Stamp Redemption Center. Mickey told his mom where we were going and in an unexpectedly good mood she gave him money for us all to get coffee cabinets at the Newport Creamery next door to S&H.

When you are between the ages of ten and fifteen, there is always a feeling that any adults around you think that you are up to no good. In our eyes, every adult's head turned and looked at us with suspicion as we entered the Green Stamp Center. We immediately thought that the store detectives would descend upon us, accusing us of some indefensible crime which would land us in the Sockanosset Boys Training School, where unspeakable things would happen, keeping us away from our parents for the rest of our lives.

I saw that suspicion in Audrey's eyes as I approached the counter with the order form and my hard-earned Green Stamp books in hand. Audrey was around our parents' age, which of course meant that she was one of "Them." She had reddish hair that went well with her Plaid S&H apron and rose-rimmed glasses with a neck chain that I'd only seen on the nose of my two grandmothers. She looked at me over the rim of those glasses as I handed everything over to her. I immediately thought of Mrs. Hoboken from the school cafeteria. Mrs. Hoboken doled out precise pieces of shepherd's pie to each student - no more, no less. If you were to ask for a little more gravy or cranberry sauce, she looked over the rim of her glasses at you in that same way.

Audrey had a little red rubber hood over her thumb that was supposed to help her rifle through the stamp book pages efficiently. Even with her neat little thumb doodad in place, she used the old-school method of licking her finger before going through each stamp book. I waited patiently, staring at the "Hello, I'm Audrey" button pinned to her apron. I could feel my face growing hot for no reason while Mickey and John tried to make themselves as small as possible behind me. When she was finished counting the books, she tore out three pages from one of them and returned it to me.

"You have a little extra here. Use those next time."

With that, she stamped and signed my order form. She gave me a nice smile and told me to take the form to the distribution area in the back and they would take care of me.

The distribution area was basically a square hole in the back of the store with a big conveyor belt and one of those vacuum tube systems that we always thought our GI Joes would love to take a ride in. The guy working the counter took my paperwork with such disinterest that I illogically felt he must have worked very hard to muster up such a stoic demeanor. His name tag was pinned onto his shirt but just barely. The name on it was scribbled in and could possibly have been Billy. He popped the form into the vacuum capsule and it was whisked away. I waited as patiently as I could, thinking that now I had nothing to prove I'd brought my stamps in and if they wanted they could just send me on my way without my radio. Surely Audrey would testify to the management that I had fulfilled my stamp quota? But no, she was on their team. I stood at the mercy of adults once again with little to show for all of that stamp licking.

After a few minutes, a small box appeared along the conveyor. I could clearly see the photo of the radio on the cover. Billy picked it up and turned in the same movement, handing it to me.

"There ya go, sport."

We left the store again feeling that we might be stopped before we reached the door but we walked out seemingly unnoticed. A quick stop at the Creamery for our cabinets and we were on our way. The plan was to head back to my house, go up to the attic room that was our sanctuary, and listen to some music while we played cards. It was a pretty short walk and I kept ogling the box that contained the radio as we cut down Belmont to West Avenue. We were in great spirits with the feeling that we had somehow pulled one over on the grownups. How could it possibly be that we got a radio without paying anything for it? It all seemed too good to be true.

We were approaching Star Wine, the package store that sponsored one of our Little League teams, as well as most of the working men in our neighborhood. Suddenly, Mickey put a hand on my chest and stopped me. He pointed up the street.

"Jimmy Kelly."

Jimmy Kelly was a legend in the area for all the wrong reasons. Everything about him spelled trouble. He was an older guy, twenty at the time. He'd dropped out of Pawtucket West early and gone to work in a car body shop. He'd been in and out of Sockanosset as well as the real jail several times. The rumors we often heard varied from simple shoplifting to brawling to car theft and armed robbery. He maintained a regular presence in front of Johnny's Pizza Place and there he was, with his long unkempt red hair and scruffy beard. He was dressed in his usual attire, jeans, work boots, and a white T-shirt with a package of Lucky Strike cigarettes rolled up in one sleeve as if he were James Dean. One of the Luckys dangled out of his mouth as he leaned on his hot-rod-in-progress Plymouth Fury with its dirt-brown primer and mismatched wheels.

We knew better than to walk by Jimmy Kelly on any given day, never mind with a brand new radio and fresh cold coffee cabinets in our hands. In my mind's eye I could already see him leaning on that car, my radio in his hand as he listened to the Red Sox, waiting for Yaz to knock one "outta da park" while chewing on the straw of my coffee cabinet.

The previous summer, a group of older kids had taken my bike from me in Slater Park. That had been my first real experience with implied violence and unjust events. I knew full well that Jimmy Kelly would have my radio at the end of the day if we went anywhere near him. We turned around as casually as we could and cut up the next street back to Pawtucket Avenue.

After walking a wide circuit to give us a safe berth from Jimmy Kelly, we came up the other end of West Avenue going toward my house. We had several acquaintances on this end of the street and at the very least knew who most of the families were. Walking by Mateo's house we pondered the mystery of his family somehow getting from Cuba to Pawtucket, oblivious at the time that the move had been an incredibly difficult and dangerous undertaking.

Approaching Matt Foster's house we contemplated stopping by to see if he was home. Matt was a friend who was occasionally a part of our small circle. Matt's brother Tommy had a room set up in their attic with couches and chairs, a great stereo, bright neon posters that would glow in the dark from his black light, and a huge American flag painted on the ceiling. We had visions of setting up my attic room the same way but that would be a few years' worth of early morning soda bottle collecting and many suspicious glares from old Mrs. Conners.

Tommy was okay with us hanging out there once in a while as long as we didn't touch the stereo. He was generally a pretty cool guy to us, much better than John's brothers ever were. Tommy was just a bit older and part of the PPMF. The PPMF were a group of older kids from the neighborhood who, aside from various malicious deeds, were the self-appointed watchdogs of the area. As far as the parents were concerned, PPMF stood for Payne Park Motorcycle Fans but anyone paying attention knew what the MF really stood for. There were always stories going around about things they'd done, their initiation rites, and the secret clubhouse that had a stash of beer, cigarettes, and Playboys. Kids on our level were under their radar, which was just as well. Still, knowing a member of the PPMF was a little step up. If I had told Tommy about the Slater Park incident with my bike I'm sure he could have gotten it back, but that would have left me in their debt. I envisioned myself like one of those beleaguered working class guys that we saw in the Mafia movies at the Leroy, owing a favor to the mob boss. I'm certain that the payback would have been something impossible, like getting them liquor or smokes. They probably would have made me give them my radio. It was definitely wiser not to ask any favors of Tommy.

We decided not to stop at Matt's and walked around Payne Park, bustling with its summer activity, and up to my house. As soon as we opened the door to the downstairs hall I could hear my mother yelling on the phone. She was trying to explain to Grandpa why his hearing aid wasn't working. This was a common occurrence and the dark humor of it had worn off long ago for Mom.

I poked my head in the door on the way up to the attic just to let her know that I was home.

"I got my radio, Mom! Thanks for the Green Stamps!"

She cupped her hand over the phone and said "That's great, honey. Don't leave it where the dog can get it. There's veal loaf in the fridge if you and the boys want a sandwich."

There were three things here that stopped me and made me forget all about the radio for a second. The first was that she cupped the phone so that her dad couldn't hear her talking to me, which seemed absurd even to a kid.

The second thing was that I wondered what sort of alternate universe my mom thought she was in where we would ever want a veal loaf sandwich. I had told her over and over again how much I despised the disgusting glutinous lunch meat that had taken up permanent residence in our fridge. Veal loaf made Spam look like steak.

The third thing was what truly made me pause. For a moment I had a glimpse of my mom and the way things really were for her. I took in her posture, her appearance, the general condition of our kitchen with the ancient porcelain sink and the worn and torn, pet-stained linoleum, the second-hand kitchen set, and the wet clothes waiting to be hung on the clothesline that ran from our window. I know now that it was what they call a moment of clarity, but back then my only thought was that I should be a good kid for her. She *needed* me to be a good kid.

"Okay, Mom. We're headed upstairs."

Our attic room was sweltering in the summer and freezing in the winter but we didn't mind. It was our refuge. We were allowed to hang out up there and were given the freedom to fix it up the way we wanted. The only hard and fast rule was that we couldn't sleep up there. It was a safe place for us away from the dysfunction of our families. We laughed, fought, and had some very serious conversations up there not usually typical of teens.

After opening the door into the superheated room, Mickey immediately went to open the window. John got the cards out as I opened up the radio. It came in a shiny blue and white box. I knew it was a good one because it was a Motorola, the same brand of TV that my grandparents had. On the box it said "*Real* transistors!" That made me wonder if any companies made radios with *fake* transistors. The battery was included which was a godsend, saving me from having to go downstairs and rifle through the junk drawer for a nine volt battery. It had a leather binding around the edge, a display of frequency numbers and graphics that I can only describe as a very serious grown-up look, and a great retractable antenna that could turn in any direction.

John dealt the cards and I turned it on.

It's not that we never got to hear music back then. Our various siblings listened to it all the time and we were getting a sense of what we liked already. But this was ours. We could listen to what we wanted when we wanted as long as we wanted. We even heard Yaz knock a few "outta da park." Although future years would bring us bigger, better radios and even our own stereos, that little box gave us a few golden moments that I have never forgotten. The thought of it always makes me smile.

A lot of other things happened that summer. It was the summer that we found the bike down by the river and rebuilt it. It was the summer Jimmy Kelly went back to jail and the PPMF stepped up their game. Downtown the big shiny new Apex store finally put the Grants and Woolworths under. It was the summer that I noticed

Nancy Thompson in the playground and Barry came back from Vietnam. It was the summer that Mickey and John stole a beer from Mickey's fridge and took turns drinking it while I kept watch.

It was the summer before my dad got sick.

And it was the summer that our dog Phinny chewed up my radio.

ᑕᑐ

**Rick Billings** is an artist, writer, children's book author, avid cyclist, and aspiring musician. He has written and illustrated two children's books: *The Tragic Tale of Mr. Moofs* and *Melba Blue*. He has also released a collection of his published Firefighter cartoons titled *Who Took My Toast?* based on his experiences as a Firefighter/EMT.

Rick currently resides in the wilds of Barrington with his wife Kathy and Nala the wonder dog (but he will always have a place in his heart for his hometown of Pawtucket).

"Green Stamp Summer" is a true story. The names of those mentioned have been changed as well as a bit of the neighborhood geography to ease the flow of the story.

You can contact Rick at bear59dog@yahoo.com

# Farewell to Eggroll & Jazz

## For John Chan of Chan's Fine Oriental Dining - Woonsocket RI

*By Connie Ross Ciampanelli*

We gather as family
to celebrate our own John Chan,
who as a young man had a dream
to marry his loves:
music, food, and friends.

Eggroll and Jazz were the elements,
then Blues became part of the mix.
He brought us the finest musicians
from home in Rhode Island
and from the greater world
to entertain us with their gifts and grace
on musical nights.

For decades we reveled in melody,
Jazz and Blues and more.
Heard singers and trios and larger bands,
living, breathing music
that lives still in our hearts and souls.

We gather as friends
to thank John Chan
for many years of good times.
Musicians especially are grateful,
so too are countless fans,
those here, those gone.

These unique times sadly are ending, and as they do
we wish John happy, peaceful days in retirement,
precious time for art and for golf
and for joyous, priceless moments with family,
and always for music, too.

We salute you, John.
We bid you farewell,
and wish you rewarding years ahead.

ଔ

*Chan's Fine Oriental Dining in Woonsocket RI has been serving Chinese-American fare since 1905. Initially named New Shanghai Restaurant, the Chan family renamed it Chan's Fine Oriental Dining when Ben Chan purchased the restaurant in 1965. Ben's son John took over the reins, and has been booking jazz musicians, later adding blues, for over forty-five years. The closing of this iconic Rhode Island institution will leave a gap in the local live music world.*

**Connie Ross Ciampanelli** is a writer from North Providence, Rhode Island. She earned her B.A. from Rhode Island College. Married for forty-five years to Anthony, the mother of two grown sons and grandmother of two, she is now retired.

Connie is the author of two non-fiction books, *Journey to 10: Adventures of an Older Novice Runner,* the story of becoming a runner at age fifty-nine, and *Bart the Mysterious,* about a feral cat that Connie and her husband took care of for nearly twelve years.

# Narragansett Bay

*by Deborah Katz*


The scent of the salt of the sea
was brought to me
by the breeze of Narragansett Bay.
While on our family's screened porch, I would sleep the night away.

Off Narragansett Boulevard, in old Cranston's peacefulness, I lay
Until the sun of a bright new day.

Down the road, a Warwick bike ride away
Gaspee Point's historical "Burning of the Gaspee" display,
A place for a picnic lunch on the rocks with friends
where ever-present seaweed air descends.

South, along the coast, Wickford adds to the bay,
July Fourth fireworks and a Wickford Arts Festival – first-rate, I
          would say.

Farther south still, Narragansett Pier Beach
Where my hubby and I did first meet.
He sure looked cute - I guess he thought the same,
"I'll see you when you're older," he said, after asking me my name.

Many a wave I rode at Narragansett Pier
and, something else I couldn't believe I did one time there.

Hanging out not far from the shore
with a group of friends, laughing and jokes galore;
Before I knew it, I was sitting on the shoulders of a friend

Standing chest high in the water, he had scooped me up to that end.

And then -
I was further surprised again!

Facing me was another girl on the shoulders of a guy,
She had her hands out, up high.
The game I had become part of was to arm wrestle with another:
Only one would stay up high, and off into the water for the other!

This group of young people had a certain area, for you to add your
    beach towel to theirs,
Many a time was spent in the summer, singing to the guitar of one
    of the peers.
The members of the young teens to mid-teens group varied from
    time to time,
But the place to add your beach towel seemed to have an invisible
    'Welcome' sign.

In between Wickford and Narragansett Pier Beach, along the coast
    of Narragansett Bay,
Is the Bonnet Shores Beach Club on the way.
Until age about twelve, my family went to the original Bonnet
    Shores Beach Club
It was nature's cozy place, not at all as elaborate, nor expensive, as
    today's version sub.

While at 'Bonnet,' our family survived the side effects of '54's Hur-
    ricane Carol,
Side effects on the character of the water, ahead of the actual hurri-
    cane's barrel

I, at nine years old, and my mother, Marvelous Millie, felt the mud
    beneath our feet disappear.

A trench had been created, and we were pulled to safety by a man
    thankfully near.
My father, out far, had been thrown a floatable life ring,
My brother body surfed a wave to shore. "Aqua King!"
At Bonnet, I also survived my beach walk with Susan Creamer
We followed the shore, but for our return, high tide had dealt our
    path a beamer.
We had to climb a cliff to return
Then laughed so hard, salty tears hurt our sunburn.

For many years, my husband and I and our two sons
Spent many enjoyable weekend beach runs
Narragansett Pier Beach has been our first choice
I think it has the best water, best sand, and, at its juncture with Nar-
    row River, piping plovers get their first voice.

"Little Rhody" and its Narragansett Bay
Have many more places to swim, eat, and play.
But a very simple pleasure would be
sitting on the Narragansett Beach shore, having salty-tasting water
    roll over most of me.

☙

**Deborah Katz** is a Rhode Islander with a Boston University
B.S. and two U.R.I. Master's degrees in Education and in Counseling. She has always enjoyed writing, especially poetry, since a child.

Deborah wrote and illustrated *Dorsey*, a book about a dol-
phin, a favorite with her classes for many years. She plans to self-
publish the book in multiple formats, so it will continue to bring
hope and smiles to many children.

Deborah has extensively researched nutrition and health sub-
jects for decades. By self-publishing a unique cookbook, utilizing

some of that information, she hopes to benefit the health and outlook of others.

Deborah's poetry and non-fiction have been published in two of ARIA's anthologies: *Under the 13th Star* and *Selections*.

Over the years, music has found its way into Deborah's writings. It still does. Keep your eyes open and your ears tuned.

# The Magic of WaterFire

*by Laurie Heyden*

**C**ome forth, people of all towns and nations, and grace my riverfront with your presence. I, Providence, welcome the world to my celebration of humanity, art, music, and culture. Gather around the warm firelight of my sparkling bonfires and exhale a sigh of surrender. Now is the time to lay your burdens aside and renew your spirit. This enchanting, transformative evening is my gift to all who accept the open/standing invitation.

Join us, people of all tribes and lands, and charm my waterside with your diversity. You are each an irreplaceable facet of the priceless gem we call humanity. Open your heart to a rich sense of belonging as you lounge together in friendship around my flowing waterway of radiant firelight.

Watch the celebration begin as the mesmerizing flame dancer sets ablaze the linear installation of wood-filled cauldrons. WaterFire is a living, breathing, moving art form where every participant adds a stroke of beauty to the composition by their presence. Be energized by the intersection of fire and water, darkness and light, art, and culture. Allow the entrancing music from distant corners of the Earth to resonate within you. From Reggae to Arias, Operas, Waltzes and Merengues, let the melodious sounds from across the globe awaken your spirit. From bongos to guitars, pianos, and violins, let the acoustic vibration pluck the heartstrings of your soul. Be mindful of your heartbeat as it slows to synchronize to the beat of the timeless music. Let the aromatic scent of burning wood take your mind to a place of serenity. Bring your attention to the present moment as the reflection of the red-orange flames shimmer in unpredictable patterns on the cool water.

The hands of Father Time are pinched, as the past and present find themselves in a dynamic tango of old and new, darkness and light, timeless tradition and modern living art. Engage in the mesmerizing ancient ritual of gazing at fire, just as our ancestors did in the most primal of times. Reach out to catch a lovely flower tossed to the onlookers by the theatric personification of the Statue of Liberty as she sails gracefully downstream, disappearing under stone city bridges. Lose yourself in space and time as you watch blissful companions create memories in elegant Venetian gondolas as they throb rhythmically along the water, moved by the athletic power of skilled gondoliers. An ample fleet of wood-filled boats that are named for Greek gods work tirelessly on scene through the evening, sailing back and forth. The careful hands of resolute volunteers feed generous blocks of aromatic wood into the blazing cauldrons all through the evening. Large decorative stars glowing in bright indigo lights are perched above bridges and paths, forming a striking contrast to the hot fiery flames, and adding magic to the ambiance.

Now is the time to refresh your spirit. Allow your senses to be filled with joyous sights and ethereal sounds, as the stress upon your shoulders evaporates slowly into the smoky haze. Let your lungs fill slowly and rhythmically with life-giving oxygen. Embrace the experience of this modern-day community ritual where all belong, and let joy transcend your spirit.

The truth is simple. Being with people has a power to bond, a power to heal. Being with people is a simple but potent remedy, and an underestimated necessity in a fractured world. In the light of my glow, embrace the common ground that you are already standing on. Tonight, in the togetherness and unity of WaterFire, let the obstacles to peace fade away. As good times are shared, WaterFire unites vast crowds with a simple power of friendship through the honoring of cultural traditions.

As people are magnetically drawn around my riverfront of sparkling bonfires, may all in presence experience a comforting energy, like a warm hug from the universe. Celebrating culture through international music, art, and dance nurtures an appreciation of diversity. Cross-cultural bonds are strengthened. Cultural traditions are sampled through parcels of sound, sight and moving art. The foreign becomes a little more familiar. The seedlings of new familiarity grow into appreciation, understanding and respect. Collective friendships are formed by sheer proximity and presence. A recognition surfaces that we are all a part of the same Earthen community.

WaterFire is a magical moment of unity. As the light of flickering flames dances upon the elegant countenances of all the spectators, may they see in themselves and each other a sense of unity with all of humanity. Let simplicity prevail. We are more alike than we differ. People stand among fellow seekers of a leisurely evening of joyful diversion from the daily grind. No matter the language, skin color, ethnicity, or economic circumstance, the participants of WaterFire are seekers of joy. Like in ancient primitive campfires, as people gathered to share their art forms of storytelling, today, at WaterFire, stories are shared through the experience of music, art, dance, and cultural tradition. A collective sharing of cultural traditions builds connection and friendship. A revelation emerges. Human interdependence sustains us. Contribution gives us purpose. All benefit from human connection, a basic human need.

On this magical night, as people stand peacefully shoulder to shoulder, let the invisible barriers to inclusion slowly dissipate. Let the triviality of that which divides us diminish in this magical moment of unity. The power of togetherness is the capacity for bonding. All people need and are worthy of warmth, joy, and human connection. All people are worthy to give love and receive love. All people matter. As unfamiliar faces from all lands harmoniously surround my city's riverfront, may the healing power of togetherness soothe the human kinships fractured by history, turmoil, and misunderstanding.

In the haze, a clarity prevails. A paradoxical beauty of life endures. Despite life's disappointments and sufferings, in this moment, there is hope for peace. The universe provides. Like in ancient campfires, the glowing light nurtures the souls of the people and draws them closer. The ambiance of fire, music and artistic expression is ambrosia for the soul. The magic of this evening melts the stress, rebuilds the weary and fortifies the strong. Healing the humanitarian scars of time begins. We can be this way, peacefully together, tomorrow too, led by the light of our own goodness.

I, Providence, envision the best for my people. This is my prayer.

In this moment, let a seed of possibility be planted in people's hearts for the deeper connection that is possible among humanity from this day forward. May my people have the courage to connect with one another, the patience to listen before judging, and the discernment to see into each other's hearts. May they be free to express the beauty of their inner selves. May they embrace their personal power and take the risk to share their personal gifts with the world. May the strong nurture the weak. May all my people experience the warmth of human connection and the redemptive healing of listening and understanding. May my people embrace common ground and see that they are stronger together. May the power of interdependence be acknowledged, respected, and embraced as a solution where everyone benefits. May my people experience the beauty of living fully: listening, sharing, trusting, connecting, dreaming, and loving.

Waterfire has a simple but magical healing power. WaterFire is togetherness. Togetherness is the hope of the world. The people around my modern-day campfire are, in this moment, a joyful example of peace and cross-cultural friendship. People of all races, ethnicities, economic backgrounds, and challenges are together, experiencing a moment of friendship while centered around a fire that breathes warmth and light into our souls. WaterFire is unity, peace, and healing. WaterFire nurtures cross-cultural acceptance and plants a seed of altruism. While the fires burn in the cauldrons, we are one human family together. The unity nurtured by WaterFire mirrors what is possible in the world: respect and enjoyment of other cultures.

Waterfire has a transformative capacity for peace. Let those who come to my light find the light within. May they continue to nurture this friendship tomorrow, through gentleness, love and understanding with all people. Peace is a possibility, and Waterfire is the catalyst. Let us co-exist respectfully, each shining their own light.

Strengthened by this human experience, may those who come to WaterFire carry a light within themselves: a light of love, hope, and peace. As the embers of my cauldrons dim, may my people acknowledge their own inner light found through self-reflection in this transformative event. The light of humanity is love. It is a light that was always there, deep in each precious human soul, and tonight rekindled, nurtured by togetherness, energized by friendship and connection.

May the hearts touched by the WaterFire experience go and be a beacon of hope, love and understanding. May they go and be the light for each other. Like a candle that easily spreads its light to another candle, may gestures of respect and friendship be extended from my glowing riverfront in all directions as spectators find their way home to all corners of our dear planet. May they each embrace the possibility that peace can begin with a single person, and that even small gestures of kindness and respect matter. Peace is amplified by gratitude for interdependence. Whether my people come from near or far, may WaterFire's warm glow of friendship return home to the countless communities of spectators. May peace and friendship be extended from my city in all directions, to all cities, states, and nations.

෩

**Laurie Heyden**, M.S., is a school psychologist, entrepreneur, artist, and author. In 2020, she co-authored *Peace by the Sea: Inspiring Images and Quotes to Light Your Way*, an elegant compilation of timely principles for living your best life, including her favorite mindfulness strategies.

# Laurie Heyden

Laurie is a graduate of the Johns Hopkins University and the University of Rhode Island. She has worked as a school psychologist for twenty-six years. She enjoys teaching coping skills in the Bristol Warren Regional School District and believes that social-emotional skills are as important to personal success as reading, writing, and math. Her personal mission is to be a catalyst for positive change by empowering others to find, develop, and use their gifts so that they can live happier and more fulfilling lives. Laurie's motto is "Our talents are God's gifts to us, and what we do with them is our gift to the world." She helped launch the Bristol Health Equity Zone's "Bristol Kindness Project" in 2018, a grassroots effort to spread messages of hope, love, and encouragement in the local community. She has operated her small business, "Art of the Gem", at local artisan markets for 14 years selling jewelry she designs with beads from around the world.

# Murder at the Foxy Lady

*by Steven R. Porter*

I was exhausted. The day had me questioning everything. And now, two police officers that looked like identical twins stared down at me as I sat hunched over in a metal folding chair in the corner of their depressing, humid, empty interrogation room in Providence, Rhode Island.

"Look kid, we're tired of asking you the same question over and over again. Tell us now, we need to know. Who pulled that trigger?"

I paused, took a deep breath, cleared my throat, and then gave them the only truthful answer I could.

"I just don't know."

The officer on the left scowled, then pointed the brim of his hat at me.

"That answer is getting old, kid. Save your B.S. for the girls at the strip club. You know exactly where the murder took place, you know where the body was found, and you even know the exact model of gun they used and the caliber of the bullet. Yet despite all that detail, you expect us to believe you don't have any idea who pointed the weapon and pulled the trigger?"

My mouth opened again but nothing came out. Then I began to chew on my right thumbnail. But who could have done it? I closed my eyes and flipped through a Rolodex of colorful locals I had stored in my mind to see if I could find one of them to pin this murder on. But I was just too tired to concentrate. My thoughts were all mixed up and melding together. I just wanted to be left alone and forget everything for a while.

"That's right… I just don't know. I'm sorry, okay? If I knew right now, I swear, I would tell you. I would tell everyone. Really, I would." My voice sounded more desperate than before, more hopeless. I could tell the officers were in tune to my anxiety.

The officer on the left rubbed his square jaw while the officer on the right massaged the back of his thick wrinkled neck. I could tell they were frustrated, too, and I assumed they were thinking about what they were going to do with me. The officer on the right spoke next.

"Well, kid, let me tell you this. We didn't ask to be here either. This is our job. And since I don't have any legal reason to detain you longer, I'm gonna let you go. But the minute you're ready to tell us the whole story, you better find your way back here to see us. And don't leave town. Got it?"

"Yes, officer. I understand."

"Remember, we'll be here... waiting for you."

Boy, did I need a stiff drink. The throbbing in my forehead that started right after the murder was getting worse. The walk from the Providence Police Station to the fabulous and legendary restaurant row on Federal Hill was only a few short blocks, but the humid August air made the stroll feel like a hundred miles. It was twilight, and the orange sky to the west over the highway provided a vibrant end to what had been an unproductive and frustrating day. I dragged my feet along the overpass and paused under the great gateway arch that welcomes passersby to the neighborhood. The arch features a large, sculpted pinecone hanging from its center, yet some insist it is a pineapple. I stared at it for a few moments and couldn't even figure that out. It was supposed to be a symbol of welcoming and hospitality, I was told. But considering the esteemed avenue had been the epicenter of New England organized crime for decades, that was hardly a comforting thought. Who, exactly, were they welcoming anyway?

As I turned the corner and stepped onto the strip, the summer air, heavily perfumed by frying garlic and tomatoes, hit me hard. It reminded me of exactly how hungry I was. But I was flat broke —

a stereotypical starving artist I guess — so dinner at one of the dozens of fancy Italian joints that lined the street was out of the question. I couldn't even afford the beer I was about to consume, but on an empty stomach, along with a shot of cheap tequila, I figured should be able to achieve the mild buzz needed to relax my frayed, quivering nerves.

Young, thin, Italian-looking men in black suits stood at the entrance to each of the restaurants I passed. They had the look of real mafioso stereotypes, both welcoming yet intimidating. I think people like that about the Federal Hill neighborhood. It has a great backstory. It is a place where you can make believe you are dining among elite organized crime figures yet stay completely safe while you scarf down your personal pound of pasta. It's sort of like believing Cinderella was a real queen when you visit her castle at Disneyland. It was all part of the image.

Someone opened a swanky new hookah bar where a restaurant called the Blue Grotto used to be. My hope was no one would recognize me there, but of course, I was wrong. There is nowhere to hide in these small New England communities. It's a tight neighborhood where everyone knows everyone has a hand in everyone else's business. I'dd barely stepped through the front door of the joint when Vincenzo the bouncer stopped me in my tracks.

"Well now, look who's here," he said, folding his hairy, muscular arms across his chest. "You got a death wish or something?"

"Look, Vincenzo. I won't be any trouble. I just want a quick drink. Then I'll go."

"And why should I let you in here? Did you snitch to the police and give them what they needed?"

"I am not a snitch. But I gave them everything I could."

"So, who did you pin the murder on?"

"Nobody. I swear. I don't know who did it."

"Well, that's just great. I guess that means none of us are safe now, doesn't it? Everyone on the staff here thinks you're going to finger one of them on this."

"Oh, come on, Vincenzo. I wouldn't do that to them. You know me."

"Yes, I know you all right. I know you don't have any money. I know you're unemployed. I know they're trying to evict you from that small one-room apartment over the bakery. I know you walk these streets all day talking to yourself. I know you smell like something my dog squeezed out on the sidewalk. And I know you're hung up on that Portuguese bimbo who dances the early shift at the Foxy Lady. Why wouldn't you blame one of us. What do *you* have to lose?"

I wasn't looking for a fight. But before I could respond and defend myself, I felt Vincenzo's hands on my back, then felt my body soar through the air, bounce off a mailbox and land in the gutter along the curb, a gutter filled with an impressive variety of swill — from cigarette butts and empty nip bottles to the remnants of a rotting three-day old prosciutto and cheese sandwich. Now I really did smell like crap. I landed on my right forearm which was now scraped raw from my wrist to my elbow. The blood, mingled with summer sweat, oozed slowly and I wiped it off on the front of my jeans. I was furious. My mind immediately shifted to revenge. I considered all the ways I could get back at Vincenzo. But first, I needed that drink. And I knew exactly who I needed to talk to.

The walk from the old Italian Federal Hill neighborhood to the strip club took about a half hour, and the cooling evening temperatures made the trip almost tolerable. From the street, the flashing neon signs of the Foxy Lady appeared to be something peeled off the Las Vegas strip, not the type of place you'd expect nestled in a blue-collar New England city like Providence. It was early, so inside customers were just starting to assemble and take their seats along the stage. The girls on duty all looked alike to me. Each had a wild mess of bleached-blonde hair and wore some sort of lingerie assembly that glowed fluorescent in the dim black lights of the club.

But I wasn't here for them anyway. I was here to see Mercedes. She worked the long shift on Thursday night, staying through until closing, grabbing a catnap in her car, then strapping on her high heels again for the Friday morning six a.m. *Legs and Eggs* show the club had become famous for. I never understood how strippers and pancakes went together, but somehow the Foxy Lady made it work and managed to attract a crowd every week.

I snagged an overpriced beer from the bar and sat at a table in the back corner where Mercedes eyed me right away. The corners of her mouth arched up into a perky smile as she strolled in my direction, her hips swaying right to left in a clumsy rhythm. She had shoulder-length black curly hair, was shorter than the other girls, and looked a little silly walking toward me in eight-inch spiked high heels — like a baby giraffe awkwardly walking alongside its mother for the first time, expecting to topple over at any moment. Her olive-skinned complexion looked lime green under the club's lighting, and up close, she was actually plain looking, more like the girls who ring you out at the Stop & Shop than what you would imagine to be a high-class stripper. Before things got busy, she could get away with sitting with me for a while without her jerk of a floor manager harassing her.

"Come here often, kid?" she teased.

"You know it, babe. Just to see you."

She snatched up my beer glass, swallowing half its contents in one gulp. Then, after a very hardy and unladylike belch, she sat down and crossed her legs. Her black Portuguese doll-like eyes stared straight into mine.

"So, what is it this time, sweetie? she said. "Hey… are you hurt? You are! What happened to your arm?"

"It's nothing. Just a few scratches," I said, pulling my arm away from her.

"It looks awful. It has something to do with the murder, doesn't it?"

I waited before answering. Everything had something to do with the murder now. It consumed me. It was an obsession I just couldn't shake.

"I'm just trying to work things out in my head, okay? I'm trying to figure out everything that happened and why."

She moved closer and whispered, "But you do know who the murderer is, don't you?"

"No. I keep going over the scene in my mind. I see the out-stretched arm. I can see the handgun pointed at the girl while she's dancing. I see the first bullet strike her in the chest. I see the second bullet hit her in the throat. I even see the third bullet ricochet off a speaker behind her and hit the stage, sending a plume of wooden shards into the air. I see the blood. I hear the screams. I watch as her life evaporates into thin air even before her listless body hits the worn, sticky dance floor. I see the chaos of patrons, dancers, and staff running in a dozen directions at once. There are bottles break-ing, chairs topple over. I even see the shooter leap over the bar and head through the back door and disappear out of sight."

"So you *did* see the murderer! Then you know who it is!"

"I just can't tell for sure."

"Well, at least tell me if it is a man or a woman?"

"I said I don't know!"

"How could you not know? You've described everything else? Keep concentrating. This is important!"

Now Mercedes was getting on my nerves. She sounded like those two single-minded cops back at the station.

"Look, Mercedes, I came here because I like you. I had hoped you could help me to try to calm down and focus, and here you are getting my stomach all tied up in knots again."

"So is that all I'm here for, to make you feel better? Is that how you see me fitting into your world? I want to know who the murderer is as much as anybody. That girl who died, she was a friend of mine, you know. We all knew her. She has a lot of friends in this club and they are all waiting for answers. I am frazzled, and here I look to you for help and you abandon me. I think I'd respect you more if you had come in here to calm my nerves and reassure me nothing else bad will happen."

Mercedes' insult hurt me. I wasn't sure how to respond.

"What do you mean... you don't respect me?"

"Why should I? Have you ever shown me an ounce of respect since the day we met?"

"Of course I respect you. You are very important to me."

"Oh, am I?" Mercedes stood and leaned forward. "From what I can tell, I'm just a collection of hair, breasts, eyes, and hips to you. And Mercedes is just my stage name. Besides, if I am so important to you, then what's my real name?"

I wanted to cry. I didn't know that either. I have to admit that it had not occurred to me until now that she had one. There was so much I didn't yet know about her but wanted to. And I needed to accept the fact that I was the only one who could resolve this mess. Enough was enough.

Alone, I walked into my tiny apartment and flipped on the light switch, surprised again that National Grid had not yet turned off the power. The neighboring building obstructed my view, but I could still see enough out my lone window to watch the diners still walking the avenue even at this late hour. They all seemed so full of joy. My soul swelled with self-loathing and guilt. The contrast only made me feel worse.

I sat at my desk and turned on my computer. The blue light made my eyeglasses glow, and the reflection in the screen gave me the appearance of being possessed by a demon. I started to type. The complicated plug of thoughts and emotions I had battled shot through my fingertips into the keyboard and onto the screen like magic. Mercedes deserved a real name and a backstory so I would give them to her. *Rosalie*, I thought, sounded cute. It was, after all, the name of my first real girlfriend back in high school. And I would make her taller, prettier, and smarter, too — she deserved that. I would portray her as a talented out-of-work actor with a heart of gold, down on her luck, caring for her ailing mother, stripping at the local club to make ends meet. And those two cranky police officers needed names, too, as well as more distinct personalities. How about Martino and Fitzpatrick? One of them will be posturing for a promotion while the other will be corrupt. After all, this will be a Federal Hill novel.

But most of all, I needed to solve the murder. After the night I had just endured, that decision was easiest of all. I decided that Vincenzo the bouncer at the hookah bar will pull the trigger in a jealous, psychotic rage. It fit the personality I had created for him. Vincenzo will believe that if he can't have her, no one will. That bastard.

I typed all night and now the sun was rising. The night felt so short, and I had yet to sleep at all. I flopped into my unmade bed and stared up at the stained, cracked plaster on the ceiling. I had to find rest. Tomorrow, I would walk the streets again, this time with the mayor. And I know he would have a lot of questions.

ᖉ

**Steven R. Porter** is the author of two novels: the critically acclaimed Southie crime-thriller *Confessions of the Meek & the Valiant*, and the award-winning historical novel *Manisses,* inspired by the rich history of Block Island. He is also the co-author of *Scared to Death… Do It Anyway,* a guide for individuals who suffer from anxiety and panic attacks.

Steven speaks frequently to schools and libraries about his books, trends in independent publishing, and on special topics in writing and book marketing. He served as Director of Advertising and Public Relations for the 176-store Lauriat's bookstore chain through the 90s, and today, he and his wife Dawn own Stillwater Books and the independent press, Stillwater River Publications, in Pawtucket, Rhode Island. He is also founder of the Association of Rhode Island Authors (ARIA).

# A Flurry of Winter Memories

*by Kara Marziali*

Our new house was built on Snowdrop Drive. Not knowing that snowdrops were a type of flower, I simply thought it was an appropriate name for a street that would be blanketed by snow during the Blizzard of '78 just three months after we moved in.

I was only 9 years old — almost 10 — at the time. The historic Nor'easter that began on the morning of February 6, 1978, took Rhode Islanders by surprise. Meteorologists were unable to forecast the size and severity of the storm. No one was advised to stay home, and thousands of people were stranded on roadways as the snow accumulated around them. Even industrial plows were stranded in traffic. It snowed a record 36 hours straight and by the time it ended, more than 40 inches of snow had fallen in some parts of the state.

While the storm itself only lasted two days, we felt the effects of it for weeks afterwards. The snow knocked out power lines and I recall being without electricity or heat. Luckily, we had a fireplace and "camped out" in front of the hearth to stay warm. Dayna and I were able to snuggle up in the blanket that Nonna crocheted. She wrapped it snugly around me and my sister saying we were two little pigs in a blanket and sang a nonsensical song she made up on the spot called "Ragazze Calzone."

Despite her silliness, I remember the palpable nervousness of my mother and grandmother during this time. They were concerned about having enough food, staying warm, and the safety of family members. Since the power was out, the matriarchs of the household were unable to cook to keep their anxiety at bay. They demanded that the men remain indoors and lured them with the promise of Italian food. At Nonna's insistence, Papa stood by the hearth for hours, like a sentinel, keeping the fire stoked and waiting for a frozen lasagna to warm up, or at best, defrost.

In turn, Mom dissuaded Daddy from shoveling by offering him the Italian egg biscuits she made the week prior to the storm. In Rhode Island, there were 26 deaths attributed to the storm, which included shoveling-related heart attacks and carbon monoxide poisoning. Clearly, this was a fate the women were most worried about.

As a youngster, I was unaware of the fatalities and other horrible aspects of the Blizzard. I merely reveled in the fantasy of making snow angels and enjoying "snow days," which meant I would be able to play outside instead of going to school. In my mind, Mother Nature clearly had brought this snowstorm especially for children to amuse themselves in the open air.

When the storm finally stopped and Mom was convinced there was no imminent danger, Daddy, Dayna, and I went outside into the winter chill only to sink in two feet of white powdery flakes. I remember laughing at how the snow swallowed up my little sister with each step she took. A four-year-old simply cannot traverse such terrain, and every time she sank, I'd giggle. Then realizing my laughter echoed against a mantle of snow, I'd cackle and hoot just to hear the sound of my voice against the backdrop of the winter wonderland we just entered. At some point Daddy had to carry Dayna, and I wished he was able to tote both of us through the wall of snow.

The sport of sledding was impossible due to the depth of the snow. So, we paved a path with our chunky boots just to reach the end of the driveway. Trudging through its thickness tired me out, and everything around me was a blinding shade of white. I don't think we were outside for very long, but it was magical. The three of us played with such jubilation that day — tossing snow, slogging through it with determination, and making a corridor of snow. It seemed to me that Daddy was as much a kid as I was in those moments. As we turned to head back to the house, following the path we had made, I caught a glimpse of Mom, Nonna, and Papa watching us from the bay window. Of course, they'd be at the door once we reached the front stairs.

And sure enough, Nonna immediately picked up Dayna, putting her warm face against the rosy cold cheeks of my sister, while Papa took my mittened hand to usher me inside. Mom looked lovingly into Daddy's eyes and kissed him tenderly on the lips.

Then together my family ate lukewarm lasagna and egg biscuits in front of the fire. These are the indelible memories that stay with me more than 40 years later.

ଓଷ

**Kara Marziali,** author of *Kara Koala and Her Kaleidoscope of Feelings*, is a writer, artist, actress, and educator. Her professional skills include graphic design, marketing and communications, copywriting and editing, event planning, teaching, and leading workshops. Born and bred in the Ocean State, Kara has always been bothered by Rhode Island accents and refuses to pronounce her current city of residence as "Worrick." She remains a dedicated patron of the arts and is at her best when she's engaged in creative and expressive endeavors. When Kara is not with family and friends, you can find her crafting, painting, journaling, singing, dancing, or playing. Although she doesn't frolic in the snow anymore, she is most comfortable in environments that stimulate curiosity, cultivate creativity, kindle compassion, and facilitate connections.

# The Newport Nuisance

*by Tim Baird*

**J**umping from the seats, the four friends quickly hustled their bikes over to the side of the unassuming house on Drury Lane. Wheeling them around to a rack on the back corner, they parked the bikes and ran up the steps to the front door. Zoe, the de facto leader of their quartet, reached out to the door and gave it a quick knock. She knew that there was a camera watching the porch and that it would only open if the person on the other side trusted the awaiting guests.

Stepping back, she motioned for the rest of the crew to stand still and wait. Zoe had been inducted into the Order a while back and was informally tasked with bringing her three friends up to speed. They were still in their trial period, so they had to stay focused. She doubted that they could really do something bad enough to get kicked out, but then again, she had heard some pretty rough rumors about their leader, Lady Lucy, and how strict she could be.

Just as she was beginning to get nervous that they wouldn't be allowed to enter, she heard the buzzer ring out from the electronic door lock and the portal swung inward. Standing there before them was her mentor and acclaimed friend of dragons, Liam Tryggvison, and a woman whom Zoe had never met.

"Ah, these must be the special agents you mentioned, Liam," the woman said as she turned to face them. "I have some trouble brewing down in Rhode Island, and I need your help."

An hour later, the four kids, the woman, and her assistant were heading south on Route 146 in a minivan.

"So, you didn't want to discuss it back in Worcester as you said we were in a rush, but who are you exactly and why are we here?" Zoe asked, being the first to break the ice.

"Ah, right, sorry my lass," Bonnie replied. "My name is Bonnie Gold," she continued. "And I am the leader of the Rhode Island chapter of the Order of Draco. We're based in Newport and function similarly to how you and the crew do up in Worcester. Granted, we don't have any fancy-pants sword wielders related to an actual dragon like you guys, but we manage with what we've got."

This elicited a round of chuckles from the backseat. The kids adored Liam and looked up to him. Whenever it came time for training, research into ancient texts, or even just performing maintenance on the tower, the children hung on his every word and mimicked his actions, hoping to be like him someday.

"This fine gentleman is my second in command, Steven Silver." Turning her head to the side to be better heard, she said, "By the way, we're about fifteen minutes out. Please make the call."

"Yes, ma'am." Steven pulled his cell phone out of his pocket and quickly called one of the numbers in his contacts. "Yes," he said, into the device. "The usual. One coffee and the rest chocolate. Yes, six total, please."

Turning back to Zoe, Bonnie continued. "We're based out of the Newport Tower, much like your HQ in Bancroft Tower. Have you seen it before?"

"No, ma'am," Zoe replied. "I've never even been to Rhode Island before today."

"WHAT?!" Bonnie exclaimed. She turned back to the three children in the rear of the vehicle. Her eyes wide, scanning back and forth, she found equal confusion in the sideways shakes of their heads. "You kids have never been down here before? Well, buckle up. You're in for a treat."

Just over fourteen minutes later, Bonnie turned onto Bellevue Avenue and swung into a parking lot in front of a strip mall.

"Steven, would you be a dear?" she said, turning and handing the man several green bills. "And bring one of the whelps with you to help carry the cups."

Turning back to Zoe and the two remaining kids, she continued. "Where were we? Oh! Right. The tower. Our base is just a few streets over from here and located in Touro Park. Unlike Bancroft Tower in Worcester, which is semi-secluded up on that beautifully wooded hill of yours, ours is right out in the open. So, we needed to be a little creative with our entrance."

The kids looked back at her, clearly puzzled.

"Ooh! I wish that we had time to do a tour right now, but we are on such a time crunch," Bonnie said, trying to assuage their sorrows over not seeing the tower on this trip. "It's built below the remnants of an old Viking lookout post erected shortly after they had landed here. We've done a good job of staying off the radar of onlookers and almost blew our cover a few years back when some researchers started sniffing around and almost figured things out. A few well-placed papers claiming that it was only a mill and a couple quiet payments to make some people go away, and... voila! We have a secret base in the middle of a populated city."

Just then, the side door slid open, revealing the waiting Steven and Luca. Both were standing there holding drink trays, three drinks each, napkins, and straws.

"Ooh! Give me! Give me!" Bonnie reached out excitedly for her drink.

"What is this?" Zoe inquired, taking her cup from Luca.

This, my friends," Bonnie declared, holding her cup up like a prize on a game show, "is an Awful Awful. The most delectable concoction of goodness ever created by the hands of man. It is a heavenly mixture of whole milk, flavoring, and frozen ice milk."

"So," Stella began, right before sucking down another long sip from her straw, "is it just a cabinet, then?"

"Au contraire, my young apprentice," Bonnie said between chuckles. "You are quite an astute connoisseur of the dairy treats, I can see. But a cabinet lacks the frozen ice milk, which is what sets this deliciousness apart from the others."

Pulling out of the parking lot once everyone was buckled in and the drinks distributed, Bonnie headed east away from the strip mall down Memorial Boulevard. Several minutes later, after pulling off the road and parking at the beginning of a public beach, the crew unloaded from the minivan and piled out onto the sidewalk with cups in hand. Everyone except for Bonnie. Her cup sat empty in the console of the van.

"My friends!" Bonnie exclaimed over the sound of the crashing waves behind her. "Welcome to Easton Beach. Well, First Beach, as we call it around here."

The kids looked around at the wonders before them. Zoe's eyes settled on the line of crashing waves at the foot of a collection of mansions off to the right.

"This place is cool," she said to Steven. "Can we go climb on the rocks? I want to look for sea creatures in the water."

"Sure!" Steven replied, looking over to Bonnie and winking. "We will definitely make time for you to go explore and look for some creatures. Hopefully you don't run into anything too scary," he said with an awkward chuckle.

"Ooh!" someone exclaimed behind the group. Zoe looked to see Luca jumping up and down.

"I've heard of them before. Del's! Bonnie, can I go and get a drink?"

"What?" Bonnie exclaimed. "You just had a milkshake. Maybe later, bud. We're on a time crunch."

Giving a sympathetic look to the kid, for she loved a good frozen lemonade as well, she turned back to the group.

"Now, who has heard of the Cliff Walk before?" Bonnie asked, looking from face to face. "No one? Well, you're going to enjoy this then. Starting from the beach here, you can walk three-and-a-half miles that way and check out some of the oldest and most expensive mansions in Newport. One of them is even still partially occupied by relatives of Anderson Cooper!"

"Who's Anderson Cooper?" Giovanni asked, puzzled.

"What? How do you not know who Anderson Cooper is?" Bonnie exclaimed. "He's that handsome man on the news. His mom is Gloria Vanderbilt herself!"

"Who?" Zoe asked.

Giving up, Bonnie waved them off.

"As you can see, the shoreline is made up of large rocks protecting the higher ground from being eroded away by the relentless pounding of the waves. Without the Cliff Walk being built like this, the ocean would bombard the cliffs and retake what she sees as hers. The city of Newport and the well-to-do owners of these mansions have spent considerable time and money to put these boulders in place to protect their investments."

"So, how does that involve us?" Stella asked, looking around and raising her hand. "It seems like everything is okay."

Bonnie nodded in agreement. "You don't waste any time, Miss Stella, do you? Right, let's get to it, then." She led the kids down the beach and onto the beginning of the paved portion of the walk, walking until they had made their way past Seaview Avenue. Looking over the side, they could get a better view of the larger rocks just below. Pausing a moment while she waited for the last of them to catch up, she pointed to the rocks below.

"Approximately forty-eight hours ago we received the first of several tips from public authorities who are familiar with the special nature of our charter," Bonnie began. "Some of the officers had witnessed the incidents on their own while others had received notifications from members of the public. Thankfully, they were on the lookout for this sort of thing and told the callers some tomfoolery about aquatic creatures and to not worry about it."

"Worry about what?" Zoe whispered to Luca. He shrugged back.

"Dragons, my dear," Bonnie said, having overheard Zoe's not-so-quiet whisper. "Some dragons — recently hatched whelps, to be exact — were spotted in and around the area right around down there."

She watched the four faces look back at her in awe, noting how excited and nervous they all seemed to be. Except for Zoe. That girl was a spitfire and reminded Bonnie of herself as a young girl.

"From what we can tell, there are some baby dragons hiding amongst the rocks just below our feet," she continued. "Water dragon babies, whelps, you know, are typically active at night and have done a good job of evading our detection so far. As you can imagine, it's too dangerous to let them just continue living along the heavily travelled tourist area, so we need to find, capture, and relocate them as soon as possible."

"Relocate?" Luca asked. "What about their mom and dad?"

Bonnie's face warmed as a smiled graced her face. Touching her hands to her heart, she looked down at the young man. "Aw! You are such a dear. With any other creature, this may very well be the case. But this species of dragon lays their eggs in well-hidden locations near sources of food and abandons the eggs once satisfied that the young are prepared to hatch and fend for themselves. It might seem harsh by human standards, but the dragons have lived for millions of years using this methodology, so there must be something to it."

"So, when do we begin?" Zoe asked.

After the sun had set and the beach was cast only in the faint light from the moon, the group made their way back to the rocks. They had walked up the street to the Cliffside Inn to enjoy the tea-room and raid their pastries and snacks. Over multiple cups of tea and more cucumber sandwiches than she could count, Bonnie learned what each kid enjoyed about the Order, why they stuck with it, and what their special skills were that they felt could aid the organization. She soaked up every detail and filed them away for future use.

While this mission may seem easy compared to other operations conducted by the Order, Bonnie knew that a good plan only lasted until first contact. The second an unknown variable introduced itself and mucked up their plans, she'd need to adapt and pivot to keep things moving and ensure their success.

Creeping down the last length of Seaview, Bonnie waved the kids forward. Looking around to see if anyone was paying attention, she scooted northward on the paved walkway for about fifty feet. Scanning the area one last time, Bonnie gripped the railing with both hands and shimmied herself up and over to the other side.

"Where did she go?" Stella whispered.

"Down there, I guess," Zoe whispered back, loud enough for the rest of them to hear.

Mimicking the move of the grownup, Zoe flung herself over the edge into the blackness below. Not to be outdone, she was quickly joined by her three friends.

Ten feet below at the bottom of a grassy slope, the kids brushed the sand from their hands and knees. With the water being out due to low tide, the ground was still moist, but they didn't have to stand in the water and get their shoes too wet. Letting their eyes adjust to the low light, they took in the scene and found their leader.

"Wow!" Bonnie exclaimed over the sound of the nearby crashing waves. "You kids aren't afraid of anything, are you?"

The kids smiled, accepting the compliment in silence.

Bonnie's face went from its normal jovial display of dragon-love and adventure-enthusiasm to one of serious contemplation. It was game time.

"All right," she started, now addressing them as Order operatives. "If you look down here, you can see a gap formed between these two rocks." The woman kneeled into the sand-rock mixture and crawled toward the opening, pointing inward as she moved.

"Luca, bring up that flashlight and see if you can shed some light on the subject."

The boy laughed at her terrible pun, but secretly loved it. His father was a connoisseur of dad jokes, and he grew to enjoy the dry, often ridiculous style of humor. Crouching before the small cave, Luca pointed the light into the opening and froze as two small orbs reflected light back at him.

In a blur of red and black, a wave of colored scales and wings rushed toward the boy and knocked him back into the water. Three blue dragon whelps, no bigger than a large dog, had leapt from the opening and barreled into the still-stunned Luca. The heads of the creatures frantically darted from face to face of the equally surprised humans gazing down upon them. Three sets of stubby-clawed feet nervously pawed the ground. Then as one, they blasted off in different directions.

"Quick! Catch them!" Zoe yelled out.

She dove toward the closest one to her and came up empty as the wily creature tore through the group and zipped under Bonnie's feet, sending her hurtling to the ground. Reaching down to the woman's outstretched hand, Zoe helped her up and the followed after it, back toward the cave.

The two remaining babies zipped directly up the rocky cliffside, jumped onto the walkway above, and zigzagged down the shoreline, heading south. Without saying a word, Bonnie and the three remaining kids chased after the other dragons, leaving Zoe to catch the first.

"Come here, little guy," Zoe whispered into the dark. She was on her hands and knees crawling through the damp sand, her back scraping against the top of the tunnel as she progressed. She couldn't tell just how far she had gone, but Zoe knew that she had travelled at least twice her height by now. What concerned her, though, was that she was starting to go downward. Each shuffle forward brought her into wetter areas, and eventually, into standing water.

Nearing what had to be the end of the tunnel, Zoe could hear a new sound over the ever-present crashing of waves: breathing. Clambering around a rock jutting into the passage from the right, she paused. Up until now, she was able to see from the moonlight reflecting off the water. It was a cloudless night and a full moon, so the team was able to move about without drawing extra attention to themselves.

Reaching down to her pockets, she fumbled around looking for the flashlight which she had stowed there earlier. Feeling the button with her thumb, she pressed it and held the light before her. There, at the back of the cave, huddled a shivering baby dragon. It had its head buried into the rocks, but she could see in the dim glow cast by the flashlight that it was occasionally looking back over its shoulder at her.

Taking her time while softly making shushing sounds, Zoe crawled her way toward the scared creature. She had no idea how the little guy would react to her approach, but she needed to get him out now before the tide came in any further. Closing the distance, she brought herself within arm's reach and stopped.

Reaching out with a visibly shaking hand, Zoe extended her arm and hovered just over the small creature's back. Slowly lowering it towards the skin of the tiny whelp, she gently touched the scales just to the side of its dorsal ridges and stroked back toward herself. The whelp pulled away at first, but then allowed her contact after a very long moment. It looked up at her, and while she wasn't definitively sure, she could have sworn that it smiled.

That is, until the water crashed into them.

Shrieking in surprise as the freezing cold water lapped at the back of her legs, Zoe scared both herself and the whelp as the wave worked its way through the tunnel and splashed into them. It shot past her body and drenched the tiny creature, throwing it into a fit. She assumed that it could swim but given the multitude of stressors currently ravaging the young being's mind, the wave was probably the last thing that it needed.

The whelp shot back in response, pushing against Zoe's tiny frame, and driving her into the side wall of the tunnel. She tried to wrap her arms around it, but the waves had made everything slippery, and she couldn't find purchase on the dragon's scales. She banged her head into an adjacent rock and dropped the light, plunging her back into darkness. Reeling from the blow, she fought against a sudden feeling of stupor threatening to knock her out.

Feeling the dragon slip past her, she threw her arms out in desperation, both to grab onto the creature and find any rock, stick, anything, anything at all to grab on to and lead her back to the tunnel entrance. Regaining her composure as her brain fought through being rattled against the rock back there, she managed to see through the darkness and found the path once more. Crawling on bruised hands and knees, each advance hurting more than the last, she scurried down the length of the passage, desperately seeking fresh air and the slimy tail of her quarry.

Gaining ground on the impossibly fast whelp, she lurched forward and was just about to grab onto it when she felt a rush of heat race through the muscles of her calf and ankle of her right leg. Struggling to move forward, she looked back in the dim light to see why she couldn't move. A rock had fallen from the side of the tunnel, landing over her leg and pinning her in place. She wasn't going anywhere.

Looking forward, she could see the dragon make it to the end of the tunnel. Its silhouette was eclipsed by the reflected moonlight shining down the length of the tunnel, and for the briefest of moments, she forgot about the pain, impending rush of water, and marveled at how beautiful the creature really was. She didn't know why, and it pained her to ask for it, but she yelled for help. To the dragon.

Turning its head just as it was about to leave, the dragon looked back to her. Perhaps it was only having fun and enjoyed being chased. Maybe it was doing a victory sneer at her failure to catch him. Or maybe, just maybe, it was looking back in sorrow at her predicament. She would never know. The dragon turned back toward the beach and bounded forward.

"Sorry! Oof! My bad!" Luca blurted out a string of apologies for the hundredth time in the last five minutes. At this point, he wasn't even looking at the person to whom he was apologizing. It had simply become a reflexive action while he ran.

And boy, did he run. And dodged broken bits of antique furniture and glass, oddly enough.

After they had begun their chase of the two dragons, the four of them had quickly discovered that these dragon babies couldn't fly yet but could run like Olympic marathoners. The little guys had quickly darted down the rocky walkway due south with the Order members in close pursuit. They had passed many houses, more than they could keep track of over the sounds of their hearts beating through their chest, but they knew that they were approaching the more expensive looking homes.

While running, Bonnie had hailed Steven on the radio that they were approaching the Salve Regina campus and that they needed help.

"Try driving the dragon back toward the street," the man calmly stated over the sounds of screeching tires. "Get the dragon onto Ochre Point Avenue if you can. I'm coming to you!"

"Affirmative!" Bonnie replied. Turning back to the kids, she yelled, "Let's chase it through this yard up ahead and sweep around behind it. We need to get to the road!"

And that was when they realized the tiny yard up ahead was Ochre Court, and that Salve was hosting a festive gala that evening. They chased the dragon through throngs of people mingling on the dimly lit lawn, bedecked in their finest and holding fragile glasses and plates. Cries of surprise rang out from amongst the well-to-do attendees as the three party-crashers rushed through the crowd, throwing the scene into absolute chaos.

They pumped their legs as fast as they could go and continued the chase down the path. The dragon veered back toward the water, so Luca burned ahead on the left while Giovanni dropped back a few feet, hoping to create a tangible wedge to drive the dragon off to the right. The plan finally worked as the whelp broke off toward a humungous building up ahead.

"Go wide!" Giovanni yelled to Luca. "Let's get him to the road. I can see it just past the mansion."

"Bonnie!" Giovanni yelled out, as Bonnie and Stella had veered to the side in pursuit of the other dragon. "I think that we'll get him out to the street at this house."

"Oh no…" he heard her groan. "We're at The Breakers. Be careful… that place is expensive."

Looking ahead, the boys watched as the blue-black blur of the dragon leapt over well-kept shrubbery and launched itself through a window in the back wall.

Giovanni looked to Luca for advice and the other simply shrugged. They took off after the whelp, quickly scurrying up the side of the stone wall and through the shattered window. They found themselves in a lavish room and continued after the creature, dodging a string of smashed objects in the wake of the scaled intruder. The formerly opulent palace was apparently not designed to handle errant dragons and was now awash in broken glass and shattered artifacts.

Pushing through the mess, the boys rounded a corner as a large painting fell off the wall in front of them, landing on their heads. Carefully hoisting it from themselves by the frame, they looked down at the placard.

"Gloria and Anderson," Luca read. "Hmm. I don't know what Bonnie's talking about. That's not what a silver fox looks like." Giovanni shrugged and leaned the painting up against the wall.

Looking to their right, they saw the dragon burst through another window at the end of the hallway. Running after it, they passed through an adjacent door and outside into the spacious driveway. Heading toward the left where they felt the main road to be, they watched in horror as the dragon bound once, twice, and leapt high over the thick iron gate before them. As they watched their quarry escape to freedom, the second dragon bounded past them, leaping the fence in one bound after its broodmate.

Bonnie and Stella skidded to a halt in front of the gate, watching their dragon disappear as well. Just as their hearts began to sink into their stomachs, they watched in awe as Bonnie's van screeched to a halt on the other side. The sliding door opened and Steven rushed out, tossing a net over the first whelp just as it alighted the sidewalk before them. Before they even knew what was happening, the man deftly netted the second and gently struggled it to the ground. They hustled up and over the fence, taking their time now that the chase had thankfully come to an end.

Hands on their knees, the kids caught their breaths as Bonnie and Steven lifted the equally exhausted dragons into the back of her van and secured it in the cages.

"Great job, kids!" Bonnie said. She looked around, clearly counting the number of kids with her. "Where's Zoe?"

Pulling with all her might, Zoe struggled against the rock pinning her leg in place. While it may have only been a few moments, it felt like she had been stuck for hours. The rising water continued to lap against her and was now almost up to her shoulders. She feared that she would soon find herself with no air to breathe.

But she wouldn't give up.

Despite the pain shooting up the length of her leg, she pulled and yanked against the very earth trying to hold her back. She was breathing harder with the effort and found herself frequently being splashed in the face by a rogue wave. The salty water was freezing and sapped her of her strength, draining what little reserves of energy remained quickly. While she would fight till the end, she had to admit that the end might come sooner than later.

Tugging against the rock, her own leg acting as both her lifeline and ultimate demise, she sucked in a last mouthful of air as the water level rose above her lips. Gritting her teeth, she bent her head forward and searched the flooded tunnel walls for anything to grab on to. Finding purchase on two rugged handholds, she pulled hard against the rock, even as she felt something come down and touch upon the back of her neck.

Hauling against her immobilized leg one last time before she was sure she'd run out of air, she felt herself surge forward through the tunnel, finally breaking free of the unrelenting rock tearing into her skin. The water around her turned red as her own lifeforce pumped into the waters of Easton Bay. Slumping into the water, she couldn't hold herself up any longer. Her muscles had given all that they could, but ultimately had their limits. Feeling her body being pulled from the tunnel toward the cool night air, her mind followed suit and she passed out.

Squinting against the bright light, Zoe slowly awoke to find herself lying on her back and staring up at the underside of some type of vehicle. She tried to get up but found herself strapped down to a stretcher mounted near the feet of a handful of people. Looking around from face to face, she realized that she was surrounded by her friends. Her gaze landed on Bonnie's face as she heard the woman's voice chime in her ear.

"Good morning, Zoe," she whispered loudly. Zoe could tell that she had tried to speak quietly into her ear via the microphone headsets that they were all wearing but had to speak loudly enough to beat back the sounds from outside. "How are you feeling?"

"Strange," she muttered, looking down at her leg wrapped tightly and held in place. "What happened? Where are we? Why am I strapped down?" Her voice began to rise, panic creeping in as the anxiety of so many unknown variables assaulted her senses.

"Just rest for now, my dear," Bonnie said. "You did well back there, and everything is being taken care of. Sit tight and I'll explain everything to you when we're back on the ground."

"But what about the dragons, are they okay?"

Smiling, Bonnie looked down at the girl in admiration. Even half-asleep and in pain, the girl was still worried about her dragons. "Well, why don't you take a look?"

Bonnie turned to the pilot and gave a hand signal that Zoe couldn't understand. The helicopter slowly turned to the side, angling the craft just enough that Zoe could see down to the ground below. In the middle of the forest, a lake sat nestled amongst the shadows of the nearby mountains, completely protected from prying eyes and far enough away from any human settlements to lead to an inadvertent discovery.

Zoe looked down at the lapping waves of the lake and grinned with delight as she saw three shapes swimming through the cool, blue water. Her dragon and its two broodmates had been relocated and now had a new home of their own. She watched for a moment until the helicopter leveled out and they disappeared from view.

"Will they be safe?" she asked Bonnie.

"I think so," the woman answered. "We have some park rangers stationed nearby to keep an eye on them."

"Can I, um…" she trailed off, unsure how to ask.

"Someday soon, my dear," Bonnie replied, knowing what she was trying to ask. "We'll come back someday soon."

◌ঠ

An engineer by day and a writer by night, **Tim Baird** spends his days lost in the world of medical device design and manufacturing while dreaming of the fantastical. Volunteering with children in several youth robotics programs, he is trying his hardest to avoid growing up, one robot at a time. When he's not designing or writing, he enjoys time at home with his wife and son, watching/reading anything Star Wars related, and spending time out in the woods of New England. Tim has been writing since 2014 and has authored four fantasy novels, one science fiction novella, and a science-based children's book.

You can learn more about Tim's writing from his website, www.timbaird.us, Facebook via @timbaird.author, Twitter via @timbairdauthor, or by talking with your local bookseller.

# FALL

*by Jack Nolan*

othic was failing him. From adolescent experiment to useful resource for his life's work, doppelganger and style-guide for all his personal choices, it had seeped over the years into the marrow of Phillip Angell's bones. When had it become an addict's drug, served up habitually but without reward? This had to end — *he* had to end it — but not now! Not in the heart of its season, this dark, icy New England fall. Not when it had brought him so far as this, to the cusp of his professional triumph or his fall!

This morning he had arisen from bed to find a stranger in his mirror — complacent, slack-faced, smug, the taut lines of terror replaced overnight by soft contentment. He felt a twinge of anger in his gut, but all fear was absent, the glass reflecting only a narrowing of the eyes and a slight hint of color. He passed the bedroom quietly, lest Constance awaken with some pleasant word, then he pulled on sweatshirt and jeans, tugged on his leather boots, his raven-black caped coat and he slipped from his lair swiftly, silently.

The gray blanket of a Rhode Island morning lay close above, with sign neither of sun nor cloud nor sky to mark the presence of a heaven. Mounds of oak leaves, crisp and brown, hissed in knee-deep waves before the icy October wind and were crushed deliciously under Phillip's long strides, as they had beneath the steps of Poe and Lovecraft when each had turned his face into just such windy days as this, striding with fearful hearts the bricks and granite slabs of Providence, long years before Phillip's own birth and inevitable death. Still, this perfect setting and these familiar thoughts failed to charge him with the thrill of danger. When had death come to seem banal to him? Where was the sensation of power that dread had always so reliably fueled? He had to find these things within himself, somehow, and he didn't have much time.

The swirling depths of leaves covered a bed of acorns, crunching beneath Phillip's boots, each tiny explosion violently ending forever the promise of a giant oak. He turned his face to the wind, hurrying along a brick sidewalk laid down a century ago by strong immigrant workmen who had long since succumbed to that necessity stronger than any mortal man.

Twenty minutes later, ears and fingers numb with cold were beginning to stir the passions he needed to feed upon. A beginning had been made, perhaps. He hurried over the frozen ground in the realm of the dead, familiar ground marked by the tall obelisks and impressive mausoleums of the great families that had built the city from port to factory-town to university center, powerful men who had all gone under, along with their cherished families whose cold bones lay with theirs beneath the marble and granite, their monuments floating upon a sea of simple markers of lesser folk whose names and dates often were scrubbed from their gravestones by time. Phillip's tall, lanky frame would have made an odd sight, as he hurried through the vast realm of the dead at Swan Point Cemetery, had anyone else been present at this early hour to witness him. At length he stopped before the low, simple marking stone of H.P. Lovecraft, whose tormented struggle with his life had ended on the Ides of March in 1937 and whose legacy Phillip had inherited. Howling up the steep bank of the broad Seekonk River, torrents of freezing wind blew his hair across his face and into his eyes wet with tears that were, perhaps, only drawn by the cold.

"You fought it," Phillip spoke aloud to the bones beneath the frozen ground. "You had the courage to confront it, to face it and not to go down in numb and willful ignorance. You reached within to seize the horror and inspire those of us who need you. Help me now to feel it! Help me to gather my strength!"

"Constance!" he boomed out, slamming the door of their apartment. He was unaware that it was after midnight, that neighbors in the apartment house might be sleeping, that he had frightened her by exploding in. He had been running madly through the night for two miles, up the steep side of College Hill, blindly racing to her.

"Connie! I did it tonight! I was better even than Saturday, better than I've ever been in my life! Oh God! I reached into their chests and held their beating hearts in the palm of my hand! There was such tension in the house, absolute silence, the terror of the dead father driving Hamlet's madness so real they could smell his presence!"

"I've been worried about you," she broke in. "You were gone all day!"

"I ran all the way from the theater to tell you. I never knew I could be this good, even when Collins told me I had the talent. I'm the youngest cast member ever to play the role!"

She laughed then, dropping her book across her chest, her black curls shining in the reading light, her pretty face glowing. She imagined the gaunt, pale figure of her beloved Phillip, his cape flying behind him as he sprinted through the town, through the RISD and Brown University buildings and stately homes of the East Side, two miles in the black of night, to throw open the door and proclaim his victory. "Have you eaten at all?" she asked.

"Yesterday."

She heated soup and made him a sandwich as he sipped wine and talked of fear. "In the last act Sunday, I felt it draining away from me. Saturday matinee and evening, the power kept building in me, like there was no end to it, but by the end of Sunday I was…there was still the talking of the words, the performance. I was acting…rehearsing in front of a live audience. I thought that maybe Collins was wrong to cast me, that I wasn't ready. And then tonight, from the start, I *was Hamlet*! His terror and madness, rage and confusion were no longer his. They were *ours*! His words were coming through *me*. The skull I held was a man I had known, Old Yorick for whom I felt the sincerest grief. There was no audience, no lights, no stage, just one moment in time, then another. The audience scared me to death at the end, not only the applause but that they were even there!

"And the ovation was so intense, it ruined everything. Taking bows felt like the most humiliating, hypocritical thing I've ever been made to do, following the most real, genuine thing I've ever done. What if, when the lights came up, they had just stayed in their seats and cried... grieving for Hamlet and Ophelia and Polonius...and then gone silently away?"

"Here. Watch the soup, it's hot." She sat opposite him, reaching across to touch his arm with her fingertips. "You're a professional, sweetheart. It's what professionals do. Surgeons, professors, they all begin by pretending they can do challenging things and sometimes they do them and sometimes they fail. And over time, they get better at what they do, like you are."

"But Connie, actors are pretending. My whole life has been a search for the genuine, the true..."

Her laugh narrowed her eyes and wrinkled her nose in that way he loved. "Your whole life is what? Six years ago, you were a teenager!"

"You know it's not the audience I'm after; it's myself. I want to experience in whole what Hamlet experienced, for myself, as someone whose own life is authentic, whose experiences are genuine and not a mere performance for others to witness. And tonight, what I'm trying to say is, I took a place within Hamlet, and I was alone there. When Hamlet died, I died. But when the applause brought me back from it...with Collins and the cast all full of congratulations and praise...I wanted to remain inside the play, still with him, with Hamlet. But there they were, the audience of ticketholders."

"Eat your soup, Phillip. You should be happy to be good at what you're doing."

Phillip picked at his dinner after Constance went to bed, trying to define in words the quandary his success on the stage placed him in. The fear of acting, forcing himself to be what he was not, baring himself before others, was exactly what drew him into acting, a great niche for a lonely, Goth-obsessed youth who thrived on fear. Achieving acclaim, the adulation of fellow actors and the public, were toxins that could not only poison his hard-won definition of himself, they could undermine the passions that made that success possible. By winning, he could lose. That was what he was trying to explain to his wife and himself. Who would Phillip Angell be in a state of satisfaction? happiness? comfort? Having found Hamlet within himself, was he now expected to do it again and again, endlessly, until the well-springs of what drove him were used up and gone?

When he slipped beneath the covers on his side of the bed, he was surprised to find his wife awake. She turned toward him and nestled into his arms, placing her warm hand on his hip.

"Phillip, my love," she whispered, "I'm very, very happy for you. I want you to know that. You're finding out that you're good on the stage and I know why that can be a problem for you. But it's going to be fine, you know. It's not going to mess you up. You'll see."

He didn't answer but lay still, fearing the loss of fear itself, fighting against the welling tide of contentment that threatened the world he had built, his world…

"Phillip, my dear," she whispered, "Dr. Avery called. We're going to have a baby."

In the dark silence, an electric charge of sheer terror swept over him, up his spine, into his brain. He said, "My God," and fell asleep feeling wonderfully alive.

ଔ

**Jack Nolan** worked for a time in the open hearth and rolling mills at US Steel Corporation, Gary Works, as did his father and grandfather.

He was graduated by Ball State University in 1965 and taught for a year before serving three years with Army Intelligence. From 1967 to 1970, he was stationed at Fort Holabird Intelligence School in Baltimore and then with bilateral operations in the Mekong Delta and Saigon under civilian cover. Stateside, he was assigned to the 531st MI Company, Fort Meade, and traveled widely – including to Providence – to take part in training exercises for Army Intelligence.

In 1976, he was awarded a doctorate in history by Columbia University, where he developed the habit of never mentioning the Army or Vietnam or Intelligence work. In 2016, great friends in The Guiness Book Club of Warren, Rhode Island, learned of this chapter of his life and urged him to write about it. *Vietnam Remix* (2017) and *There Comes a Time* (2020) relive the incandescent feelings of 1967-68 and celebrate the camaraderie of young men caught up in that zany era. If you liked "Fall," a collection of Jack's short fiction is due out in October.

Jack lives with his wife, Pat, in Providence, where he is happy to receive emails at **vietnam.remix.1968@gmail.com**

# Reminiscences of
# Sunset League Baseball and Mr. Mac
*by Paul Lonardo*

Every summer, they come from the cities and towns all across Rhode Island, men of all ages competing with the beach traffic and tourists to cross the Newport Bridge to play in a George Donnelly Sunset League baseball game at Cardines Field. This quaint, intimate ballpark is considered one of the oldest in the country. The field dates back to 1908, with the stadium itself completed around it in 1936.

On warm evenings from May through August, while many people are lining up outside the pubs, outdoor eateries, and top-rated restaurants around Newport, or walking along Thames Street visiting one of the many shops, galleries, and museums, amateur ballplayers converge on the historic baseball diamond, stretching in the outfield grass and tossing a baseball around before game time, which gets underway near dusk.

Playing amateur baseball under the lights at Cardines Field in the summer is an experience that a ballplayer, regardless of their ability level, will remember for a lifetime. There is no greater thrill than digging your cleats into the dirt around home plate in anticipation of the next offering from the opposing pitcher or running down a deep fly ball hit in the outfield gap. On humid nights, when the warm air collides with cool air blowing in from Newport Harbor and the Atlantic Ocean just across the street, a thick fog will blanket the playing field like a semi-translucent tarp.

On occasion, the outfielders dissolve from the batter's view, and worse, the fielders can no longer see the batter or the ball. This surreal tableau will prompt the umpires to stop play, delaying the game, or suspending the contest if the fog does not lift. Only at Cardines Field in Newport. Or maybe San Francisco's Oracle Park, where the Giants play.

As a former amateur player myself, wearing the uniform for R&R Construction in the 1990s through the early 2000s, I had the additional privilege playing on a team sponsored by the late Ronald "Mac" MacDonald, known affectionately to all as Mac, and respectfully addressed as Mr. Mac by young players. Mr. Mac was a Newport native and local business owner, and if one of the several R&R Construction teams that he sponsored was playing, you would be sure to see him at the field, often with his dogs at his side, watching the game and talking with the coaches, players, and spectators. Win or lose, he always had a kind, supportive word to say, and you knew he was there out of the passion he had for the game and the joy he saw in kids of all ages when they were competing on the field.

Seasons change and time marches on, and over time the century-old ballpark faced many challenges and difficult times, including coming close to being leveled and replaced by a parking lot. Like the game itself, however, the historic field has endured, in part thanks to the efforts made by Ronald "Mr. Mac" MacDonald. He not only kept the dream of playing baseball at Cardines Field alive for many future ballplayers, he allowed baseball in Newport to thrive. My own playing days may be behind me, but I look forward to seeing my son play there in several short years.

Today, Cardines Field, with its quirky outfield dimensions, wooden grandstand around home plate, and congenial side-by-side dugouts, remains a grass- and dirt-carpeted oasis on America's Cup Avenue in downtown Newport. And it remains the home of the historic Sunset League, as well as the Newport Gulls of the New England Collegiate Baseball League and other local schools or baseball leagues.

This summer, they will come to Cardines Field once again, just as players have done for decades, many returning players and some first-timers. With the sad passing of Mr. Mac at the end the 2019 season, it's good to know that as long as baseball is played in

Newport, Mr. Mac's legacy will live on. I know he will be there in spirit watching the game he loved and seeing young players enjoying the unique experience that Sunset League baseball at Cardines Field offers.

03

**Paul Lonardo** has authored numerous titles, both fiction and nonfiction books in a variety of genres. Most recently, *The Legend of Lake Incunabula,* a collection of dark fantasy stories, was published in April 2022.

Paul is a member of Horror Writers Association. He lives in Lincoln, Rhode Island with his wife and son.

# The Summer of '64

*by Joann Mead*

It was the summer of 1964 when we headed out east to Rhode Island. It was a cross country adventure, along with some misadventures, as we traversed the 3,000 miles from Los Angeles to Providence. Three kids, two of us teenagers, dozed on the fold-down back seats of a shiny gold 1961 Dodge station wagon, an 18-foot ungainly beast. It was early morning in a dense fog when ten minutes into the journey a robust thump propelled us forward. With no real damage to life or limb, just a bent rear bumper and a crying little brother did little to put the brakes on the journey ahead.

Southern California, the acclaimed land of sunshine, was notorious in the 1960s as a soup bowl of coastal fog mixed with toxic smog. My persistent itchy weepy eyes gave testimony to that. The vast expanse of desert ahead gave some relief, but the unbearable heat left us drowsy, until somewhere in Arizona a honking car woke us up. At first ignored, then left in the dust, the car finally caught up with us. The driver, rolling down his window, delivered the bad news. "A suitcase blew off your luggage rack about ten miles back." On closer inspection, it was the suitcase my sister and I were to share for the month-long summer vacation. Backtracking the miles, nothing could be found— no exploded suitcase in sight, no young ladies' undies strewn across Route 66.

With stops that only warranted food or sleep and a mantra of "we have to make time," the miles droned on. Days seemed like eons until we finally made it to the promised land, Rhode Island, and to the triple-decker home located on a street with an overhanging canopy of black cherry leaves. It housed the aunties, uncles, and cousins of various generations I would get to know.

Growing up in Los Angeles, you'd need to climb winding mountain roads to see woodland trees or forests. Our Los Angeles neighborhood, conspicuously devoid of tall leafy green trees, sported only the occasional California fan palm. But Rhode Island was refreshingly green, lots of trees and the air didn't sting my eyes.

As Lady Luck would have it, we had little need for clothes in the hot, humid July and August of New England. Despite the vanishing suitcase, our replenished supply of undies, shorts, and swimming suits sufficed for the most part. And there were plenty of cousins, some a few years older than us California kids, with access to cars and friends who would show us the sights, especially the beaches. On more than one occasion, we teenagers cruised in a cousin's convertible to Scarborough and Narragansett in search of the Ocean State's best waves. It wasn't as if we California kids didn't know "the beach." Most of our summers we lolled about on the sandy Pacific beaches. Along with the "surfin'" Beach Boys, we were out there a-havin' fun in that warm California sun.

Rhode Island in some ways couldn't compete with the California we grew up in. We had our local beaches – El Porto, Hermosa, Manhattan, Playa del Rey. And we had music at the Carolina Pines Bowling alley on Wednesday nights. There was the blaring surf guitar of Dick Dale and His Del-Tones. But it was the raucous sounds of Ike, the Ikettes, and the outrageous singing and dance routines of Tina Turner — she left us shocked and awed. On Friday nights at our high school dances, we mimicked her sexy gyrating moves to the music of The Crossfires, later known as The Turtles. I always suspected it was Mark the chubby guitarist, singer-songwriter who stole lunch from my locker, more than once. For revenge, my locker-mate baked chocolate chip cookies laced with ex-lax. Our secret is finally revealed.

But only Rhode Island has the bragging rights for the Newport Folk Festival. In July of 1964, the featured artists were Bob Dylan, Jose Feliciano, Joan Baez, Judy Collins, Pete Seeger, Johnny

Cash, Peter, Paul & Mary, just to name a few. Dylan played an electric guitar—some say he was booed by Folk purists. The Newport Jazz Festival set-lists included Louis Armstrong, Count Basie, Dave Brubeck, Sarah Vaughan. Yes, Little Rhody had plenty of music greats to brag about.

I celebrated my 16th birthday that July and had little interest in going to music festivals. Like teenage girls anywhere, it was the boys of summer that drew our attention. We'd find them hanging out on "the corner" as we cruised the neighborhood. The "corner" wasn't a pastime in the LA coastal suburbs where I grew up. We'd hang out at the beach and watch the boys surf at El Porto's rocky pier. Rhode Island had few of the blond-haired youth of California. But in Rhode Island, I blended in with the darker native Italians. I'd found a place where I finally belonged, or so I thought at the time.

It would be over forty years and four countries later before I would step foot again in the state of Rhode Island. From America to London to Moscow to Zimbabwe, from A to Z and back again, eventually I came full circle. I left Los Angeles for London during the tumultuous times of the 1970s—the anti-war protests, women's rights, gay rights, and environmental movements that defined the decade. In 1979, I moved east to Moscow, Russia (back in the USSR) during the tense hostility of the cold war that lasted decades before it ferociously boiled over. It was the invasion of Afghanistan (the Soviets, not ours) that led to the boycott of the 1980 Moscow Summer Olympics. Onward to Africa and post-war independence in Zimbabwe, where in reality the war, like all wars, never really ended. They just simmer and fester before boiling over again.

As I walk with my husband on the trail at Rocky Point, I bore him with stories about the summer of '64. The signs and old photographs remind me of how it was then and what it is now. I tell Jim a story about The Shore Dinner Hall—it was the thing I remembered most. The famous multiple course dinner was a big indulgence for a group of about twenty of us. "We were warned ahead of time that we must eat everything, but not the lobster and corn on the cob. So, we ate the clam chowder, baked clams, clam cakes, potatoes, sausage, and baked fish. Also, the watermelon and Indian pudding. The next day, in yet another backyard picnic, we were served up the delicacies—the lobsters and corn on the cob."

Jim asks, "Didn't you go on the rides?" I widen my eyes, shake my head, and frown in disappointment. No, we wouldn't get to enjoy the rides. Not the scary darkness of the Castle of Terror (later the House of Horror) with its frightening giant bat, sawmill, and torture chamber. Not the spiraling thrill of the corkscrew roller coaster. Not even the gentle Skyliner ride with its bird's-eye view of the amusement park. None of the really fun stuff because... "we didn't have the time." My family never seemed to have the time or money for anything other than food. Italian memory is often about meals and food.

On arriving home to Los Angeles, a letter was found buried in the stack of mail that solved the luggage mystery. A slow-moving truck pulling a horse trailer stopped for the errant suitcase. The driver left his phone number. He lived at a farm outside of Los Angeles and would deliver it. His reward, a bottle of very fine whisky.

After our overseas adventures, life back in the US was a carousel. From the West coast to the Mid-West, Mid Atlantic, and New England, my destination in life would finally lead back to Rhode Island. And do I have any desire for wanderlust, any compelling need to move on for new adventures?

No, absolutely not.

C3

**Joann Mead** has lived in four countries ranging from A to Z: America, London, England, Moscow, Russia (back in the USSR), and Zimbabwe, Africa. She is a writer, educator, researcher, and futurist. Her written works include bio-thriller and crime novels, short stories, screenplays, magazine articles, and publications in medical journals on disasters and weapons of mass destruction. Her writing is inspired by the places she's lived and traveled and life's adventures along the way.

Her mysteries and thrillers are connected by the "underlying crimes" of genetic design. *Underlying Crimes*, her first novel, is set in a tiny New England state known for its culture of corruption. *Tiger Tiger*, her second novel, is somewhat prescient. A femme fatale scientist creates a deadly pandemic Tiger Flu virus and plots to target America. Her third novel, *Designer Baby*, is set in Scandinavia and Rhode Island. It speculates on the real and imagined possibilities of customized, gene-edited super-human babies and the creation of ethnic targeted weapons.

Her short story "Summer of '64" was selected for the 2022 ARIA Anthology. "Married in Moscow" was selected in 2020 and "A Most Unusual Proposal" was selected in 2018.

Follow Joann Mead's blog and website at www.UnderlyingCrimes.com

# Worlds Apart

*by Theresa Schimmel*

The phone ringing at two a.m. is never a good sign. It's neither of our teenage sons, who are both home and in bed. Parents perhaps? Groggily, Steve reaches for the bedside phone, while I grab the kitchen extension and return to the bedroom.

"Who did you say this was?" Steve asks.

"Mario's sister, Marissa."

"Marissa, right. What's wrong?"

"Mario's in trouble."

"What kind of trouble?"

"There's these guys outside our apartment building who are after him."

"What do you mean, 'after him,' and why?"

"It's because he's been dating this girl, Angela."

There's a pause as we wait for more information.

"Angela used to be Hugo's girlfriend and he's mad that she's with Mario now. He and his gang have been hanging out near our apartment waiting for Mario every night. They've got guns. A couple of them have AK-47's. They say they're going to kill him."

Unknowingly, I whisper into the phone, "Oh my God."

"Mario needs to get away. I was hoping that maybe he could come live with you?"

Steve looks questioningly over at me. I put my hand over the mouthpiece, and whisper, "I think we should say yes."

"Marissa, is Mario there now? Can we talk with him?" Steve asks.

Mario gets on the phone, His greeting is subdued, missing his usual exuberance. I ask, "Are you okay, Mario?"

"Yes."

I continue with my questions. "What Marissa said about the gang. Are they threatening you?"

"Yeah. Every day."

"And do you *want* to come stay with us?"

There's a pause on the other end of the line.

"Yes, I mean kind of. I don't want to leave Mom, Marissa, and my friends, but I don't want Hugo's gang to kill me." His voice is trembling.

I listen as Steve responds. "Mario, we want you to be safe, and you know how much we care for you, but if you live with us, you'll have to follow house rules, just like our boys do. You understand that, don't you?"

"Yes. I won't be any trouble."

After hanging up the phone, I lie in bed, my stomach tight. Mario's life threatened? Sleep eludes me as I toss and turn, anxious for the boy we'd come to know and love. He was ten years old when we met him. It was the summer of 1986.

My thighs stick to the passenger seat of our car as we wait in the church parking lot for the arrival of the bus, scheduled to arrive at noon. It's now ten minutes late. I glance in the rear-view mirror at my sons, eleven-year-old Kyle, absorbed in reading *Lord of the Rings,* and nine-year-old Evan, head resting on crossed arms at the open window.

I'd read about the need for Fresh Air Fund volunteer families in the newspaper. The organization arranged for children from New York City to spend two summer weeks in the country with volunteer families. Over the dinner table one evening we discussed being a volunteer family with our kids. What did they think? Kyle readily said yes, not so much because he didn't have some doubts about a strange kid coming, but because he was usually agreeable. Evan, on the other hand, was filled with uncertainty. Who was this new kid? Would they get along? Would his friends like him? Why did he have to share his room with a stranger? Yet, he was also intrigued, and, in the end, agreed.

I flip open the folder on the seat next to me, scanning again the information on our assigned child, Mario. Just the bare basics were given. Name, age, address, parents' names, and contact information. He was ten years old. It was the first time he'd been in the program. But there it was, under medical: attention deficit hyperactivity disorder. What was I getting myself into? As a Special Education teacher, I knew all about ADHD, and while I loved all the children in my classroom, after a day teaching a child with this diagnosis, I'd come home exhausted. The notes indicated that Mario took Ritalin during the school year but went off it during the summer. I sigh. It's too late to back out now.

The bus pulls into the parking lot, exhaust fouling the air, almost as if the city pollution tagged along for a ride. As the folding doors open, families cluster around the parked bus. One by one, the children emerge, each with a lanyard around their neck with their name and the name of their host family. I note the shy smiles, the slow approach of many. Only one child bounds off the bus with a broad grin. Shiny black hair curls around his ears and down his forehead. He yells back to the driver and other children. "See ya in two weeks!" They all yell back, "Bye, Mario!" *How do they all know his name?*

Introductions are made and we drive the five-minute ride home, Mario alternately glancing out the window at the tree-lined streets, the nearby pond and library, then back at my boys, who sit stone-faced. We pull into the driveway, and Mario immediately spots the basketball hoop. "Do you have a basketball? Can I shoot hoops?"

"Sure, Mario. Let's get you and your suitcase inside first."

We show him Evan's small bedroom, where he'd be sleeping on one of the twin beds. He's impressed with all the sports paraphernalia in the room, the cut-out pictures from *Sports Illustrated* glued to the wall, and drawings of MBA, NFL, and NBA sports emblems on the ceiling.

Pointing to the ceiling, he asks Evan, "Did you draw those?" Evan nods. "Wow, that's cool! I got a Mets shirt. You wanna see?" He unzips his suitcase and pulls out a folded Mets jersey. "My dad got it for me. See. Number 18. That's Daryl Strawberry. He's their clean-up hitter."

Evan smiles for the first time since Mario's arrival. "Yeah, I know. He's batting 259."

Mario grins. "That's right. You like the Mets?"

"Naw. I'm a Red Sox fan. But I follow all the stats." Evan opens the bottom dresser drawer. "Here, I emptied this drawer for your stuff. After you unpack your suitcase, I'll get the basketball."

Within minutes they're in the driveway shooting hoops. I smile as I watch them through the window before setting lunch on the deck table. The ham and cheese sandwiches are finished quickly but Mario makes a face at his first taste of clam chowder.

"Don't you like the clam chowder?" I ask.

"The what?" He'd never heard of clams and certainly not clam chowder. He takes a few more spoonfuls and announces it isn't too bad. That night, over dinner, my marine biologist husband shows him pictures of clams and other marine invertebrates, then shares stories of his clamming adventures as a boy. "We'll have to take you clamming sometime, Mario."

But for our first day with Mario, we had planned a beach outing. We choose Scarborough Beach for its expansive stretch of sand, the shaded pavilion, and available snacks. Arriving early to beat the crowd, we set out the beach blanket and chairs. Mario is wearing a yellow and black swimsuit to the knees, NY tee-shirt, and glitzy gold cross. He stands, staring at the ocean, as Kyle and Evan strip off their shirts and run toward the water. They yell for their new friend to join them. Mario sprints forward, his brown legs cycling like windmills as his feet hit the water. He dives in, jumps up, and shakes like a wet dog. Spitting profusely, he hollers, "It's salty! Why does it taste like salt!" My husband and I stand at the water's edge laughing. Mario's only immersion experience had been in crowded city pools and his swimming skills are minimal. We give him a few tips and after a while, his wild slapping stroke becomes a little more refined. The other new experience for Mario that day was Del's lemonade. It was a big hit, and I pull out another dollar for him to have a second cup.

Mario has a strong competitive streak and most days begin with he and Evan shooting hoops, tossing the football, or playing whiffle ball in the back yard. Occasionally they go across the street to a nearby field to play baseball with Evan's friends. The city kid and the suburban kids made an interesting mix. Evan and friends found Mario fun. He laughed and joked readily and was up for anything. But tempers flared when he argued vociferously over who was safe, who made a three pointer, or whether a pitch was a ball or strike. And he wasn't shy about throwing out trash talk; new to the others and not appreciated.

Finally, the day comes when I hear first the back door slam and then Evan's bedroom door. Mario finds me in the kitchen chopping vegetables for supper. He takes a seat on one of the counter stools. I raise my eyebrow and ask, "Where's Evan?" already knowing the answer. He shrugs. "In his room. Don't know what his problem is. I said we could start over."

"Problem with basketball?"

"Yeah."

"What about CJ? I thought he was out there, too."

"He went home."

I hand him a vegetable peeler and three carrots. "Think you can peel these carrots for me?"

"Okay."

I sit on the stool next to him and begin cutting potatoes. "You want to tell me what happened out there?"

He peels a full carrot before answering. "CJ is cool, but he gets mad easy. All I said was that his mother could probably shoot better than he could. And then he threw the ball at me, grabbed his bike, and left."

"And Evan?"

"He told me to stop picking on his friend. Then he left, too."

"I see." I stop cutting potatoes. "Mario, you had no way of knowing this, but CJ's mother is dead."

He sets the carrot down and looks at me. "Jeez... I didn't know. His mom is dead? How'd that happen? I got a friend whose dad was wasted last year. Then his brother."

"I'm so sorry, Mario."

He shrugs. "It's okay. We don't hang out anymore. They moved away."

"To answer your question about CJ's mother. It was a car accident. He was only five when it happened."

"I'll take it back, what I said. I didn't mean it, you know."

"Of course not."

"But Evan gets mad too sometimes. Or goes in his room and shuts the door."

"Yes, I know that about him. Sometimes he just needs some time to himself. Can you understand that?"

Again, he shrugs. "I guess."

"And I suggest you be a little more careful what you say, especially about his friends."

"I'm just messin' with him. Don't mean nothin'. I talk to my friends that way. They don't care."

I nod.

Over the course of the summer, Mario and I have a number of kitchen chats and it's in those quiet one-on-one talks that I come to know more about him. He lived in Spanish Harlem, had one sister a year younger, although from his description of her, she often played the role of big sister, watching over her brother, who, by his own admission, had a tendency to get into trouble. Spanish was spoken at home as the parents were from Puerto Rico. He told me he was rarely allowed to go out alone to play as his parents considered it too dangerous.

Knowing Mario's love of sports, we decide to make a trip to McCoy Stadium. Evan explains to Mario how he always brings a baseball in a bucket with a pen attached for the purpose of getting autographs. We arrive early and the boys, along with dozens of others, quickly run down to the front railing when the players file out of the dugout for pre-game warm-up. Some, like Mario, holler to get their attention. Others, like Evan, just keep dangling their bucket. When one of the players finally obliges, Mario beams up at us, holding his signed baseball aloft. Steve buys a game program and after the boys check out the description and stats on each player, he shows them how to fill in the innings box score card. The boys take liberal advantage of the snack bar, especially Mario, who samples almost everything. The ride home is one filled with laughter and chatter coming from the back seat.

There are many firsts for Mario that summer. Given his restrictions at home, he'd never learned to ride a bike. With a little help from us, he learns quickly and joins Kyle and Evan in regularly riding up and down our side street. Once introduced to the fun activities of mini-golf and batting cages at Narragansett's Adventureland, the boys beg to go repeatedly. I explain that my pocketbook isn't bottomless and they should try to earn some money for all these costly recreational activities.

"How are we going to earn money?" asks Evan.

"Maybe you should try selling lemonade like you did with your cousins last summer."

"But Mom, we only sold three glasses of lemonade."

"Well, maybe today will be different. It's a pretty warm day."

He moans.

"C'mon, Evan. It'll be fun!" Mario springs off the couch and runs to the kitchen. "How do you make lemonade?"

"Just so happens I bought some Del's lemonade mix the other day. You just need a pitcher, water, and ice. Evan, you and your brother can get the card table and chairs out of the garage to set up on the corner."

We live on a side street off a busy through street, so the corner was a perfect location for a lemonade stand. Mario follows my instructions in making the lemonade. We walk to the corner intersection with a jug full of lemonade and a cooler. Kyle and Evan had already set up the table with the sign LEMONADE 50 CENTS taped to the front. I walk home, figuring I had at best an hour before they'd be back with long faces and a report of few sales. Instead, twenty minutes later, Mario runs back saying they needed more lemonade. I mix it quickly and send him on his way. *Traffic must be heavy today.* After two more requests for lemonade refills, I become curious and decide to check out their stand myself. To my horror, Mario is in the middle of the road, waving his arms back and forth, yelling, "Lemonade! Stop and get your lemonade!" He is flagging down every car, rushing to the driver's window with lemonade in one hand and collection can in the other. Of course, I explain to Mario that selling lemonade in Rhode Island is not the same as car window washing at traffic stops in New York City! But I must admit they'd already made enough sales for another trip to Adventureland.

The last weekend before Mario's departure, we decide to introduce him to camping. We load up the truck with the tent, sleeping bags, assorted camping gear, folding chairs, and cooler. The three boys squeeze together in the truck's back passenger seat and we drive to Burlingame Park. As with most of the newly introduced experiences, Mario demonstrates enthusiasm mixed with perplexity. Why were we going to sleep outside? How come there wouldn't be any television?

After helping with the set-up, Mario asks if he could try fishing, like we'd promised. My husband gets out the fishing rods and shows him how to bait the hook. Dangling his worm, Mario hesitantly pierces it with the hook, then screeches, "Blood's coming out!" It takes a while before he learns how to cast, but once he does, he hollers, "I did it!" Then he waits patiently for the desired fish for all of fifteen minutes, before reeling in his line, tossing the rod aside, and announcing he's going swimming.

After a camp stove meal of hot dogs and beans, the boys collect kindling for the campfire and then search for the perfect marshmallow stick. I get out the chocolate bars, graham crackers, and marshmallows. It's a clear night with a star-filled sky. My husband points out and names some of the visible constellations, but Mario is more interested in making and eating as many s'mores as he can, tossing sticks into the fire, and asking repeatedly if any animals would get into the tent that night.

We'd hoped to go to the beach on Mario's last day but it was raining. I suggest going to Newport Creamery for an ice cream treat. Mario looks at the menu with tempting pictures of ice cream concoctions and points to the banana split. "What's a banana split?" Surprised at the question, I describe it and he immediately says, "I'll have that." I watch him dig into the split bananas, mounded with scoops of chocolate chip, peppermint, and chocolate ice cream, topped with fudge sauce. He smiles, his lips mustached with whipped cream. I smile back, already missing him.

The bus is punctual this time. Mario sits in the back seat, quieter than usual. Evan says, "Maybe next year, I can go stay with you at your house in New York." Mario frowns. "No, you can't do that. You'd get killed." Through the rear-view window, I see Evan's confused look and Kyle's frown as he puts down his book to stare at Mario. After a brief silence, I turn in my seat and say, "Mario, you can come back here next summer, and every summer after that for as long as you want." I am rewarded with what we had all come to know as the 'Mario Grin.'

As we walk in the parking lot, I give Mario a note for his parents to read about how much we enjoyed his visit. Hugging him tight, I tell him that we hope to see him next summer. He walks to the bus, then stops. The other children are all climbing onto the bus, finding their seats. Mario stands in the doorway in his white t-shirt with red letters spelling RHODE ISLAND. He gives a final wave and yells out, "See ya next year!"

141

Waving good bye that summer afternoon I had no way of knowing that our connection to Mario would continue for the next five years. He came every summer and a few other times as well when we paid for train trips from NYC during school breaks. And then there was the one visit we made to his home so that he could join us on a visit to Ellis Island.

The address given takes us into the heart of Spanish Harlem, where Steve drives among the high- rise apartments, stacked in sequence like dominoes. Upon spotting the correct building, he parks the car. A few children rush past with curious stares as we enter the concrete building surrounded by asphalt. We stand in the dark hallway and knock on 12C. Mario opens the door, greeting us with his characteristic grin. The apartment smells of fried grease and spices. A diminutive woman stands at the kitchen stove, her head wrapped in a red paisley scarf. Mario introduces his mother and then directs us to take a seat on the vinyl-covered kitchen chairs.

Setting a plate of *pasteles* on the table along with a liter bottle of Coke and plastic glasses, Mario's mother says, "*Gracias por todos sus actos de bondad. A Mario le encanta visitar tu casa.*" Thank you for all your acts of kindness. Mario loves visiting your house.

She turns away, retreating to the stove. It isn't until we finish our *pasteles* and soda that she comes closer to say goodbye. It's then I see the bruised cheek and slightly closed, discolored eye. Seeing my stare, Mario quickly kisses his mother goodbye and shuffles us to the door. "What are we going to see at Ellis Island? Will we see the Statue of Liberty, too?"

*Had Steve seen? How could I talk to Mario about this?* I couldn't, certainly not amid the tourists on the ferry or island. That conversation waited until the following summer when Mario once again sat on one of my kitchen stools and shared that he, his mother, and sister were now living in a shelter, awaiting placement in a new apartment. The escape from his father had not been easy, and they were still afraid that he might find them.

"That's why I use the name Tony now. Mario is my father's name. I don't want it anymore, and I don't want him to track us down. And I don't want to sell drugs like he does."

"Should I call you Tony now, then?"

"It's okay to still call me Mario. Don't tell Kyle and Evan, okay? Hey, can I have one of those cookies you made today?"

"Sure, take three." I watch him grab the cookies, open the screen door, and run outside. Leaning against the counter for a long time, I try to absorb what I'd just heard and imagine what it was like to live in Mario's world.

When the phone call about the gang's threats came three years later, we were ready to open our home permanently to Mario but Marissa called us back to say that Mario had decided to stay with his mother and sister. He'd broken up with Angela and was no longer being threatened.

Two years passed before we saw Mario again. Once his age made him ineligible for the program, we'd lost touch. So, I was thrilled when he called asking if he could come for a weekend visit. At first, I didn't recognize the young man who jumped from the train platform. Now seventeen years old, he was a muscular 5' 6" with a skimpy goatee on his chin. I asked after his sister and mother. It took a full year before an apartment became available, but he said they liked their new place. Marissa was a top student and was hoping to get a scholarship for college.

"And you, Mario? How's your senior year going?" I'd waited until we were alone to ask the question. I knew he struggled in school and didn't want to embarrass him in front of Kyle and Evan, both of whom were excellent students. Kyle was in his first year of college and Evan, now in his junior year, was already researching potential colleges where he might play baseball.

Mario shrugged. "Okay. Not sure I'll finish now." Before I could ask why, he reached for his wallet and said, "I wanted to show you something." He pulled out a picture and handed it to me. I gazed at the image of an adolescent girl; thick black hair pulled back from a smiling copper-tone face. A round-cheeked baby girl dressed in pink with matching hairbows and booties sat on her lap.

"This is my girlfriend, Rosalie, and our baby girl, Bonita. Isn't she beautiful? That's what her name means, beautiful."

The baby appeared to be about six months old and was indeed beautiful. My eyes watered, but I wasn't sure why. I had so many concerns, so many questions. Mario stood across from me, waiting for my response. What could I say? What should I say? I looked at him and saw the boy with the big heart and infectious grin.

"Congratulations, Mario." I pulled him into my arms and held him close.

ଔ

**Theresa Schimmel** is the author of the adult novel, *Braided Secrets,* and four published children's books: *The Carousel Adventure, Sunny, The Circus Song,* and *David's War/David's Peace,* which is used in area schools' curriculum on conflict resolution. Her short stories and poems have been featured and won awards in literary magazines and newspapers. She was a featured magazine writer for Rhode Island Family magazine for five years and current member of the Association of Rhode Island Authors, Society of Children's Book Writers and Illustrators, and South County Writing Group. She has participated in numerous writing workshops and courses. Her writing goals are twofold: to create a compelling story with appealing characters and to connect to readers, broadening their awareness of life experiences. Her books are available through her website www.tamstales.net and in some bookstores.

After twenty-six years of classroom teaching experience, she worked as an early childhood educational consultant at the state and national level. Now, she enjoys spending most of her free time writing. Married with two adult sons and three grandchildren, she resides in Rhode Island with her husband, Steve.

# Verrazzano's Enigma

*by Pete Rock*

*April 20, 1524*
*The New World*

"**C**aptain......Captain," Hugo, the first mate, called out, pounding on the door to the great cabin. "Captain, there's an island, dead ahead."

Giovanni Verrazzano glanced over at the lock on the door, rattling with every knock, knowing it would hold, but questioned what would happen if it didn't. Staring at the door until the knocking stopped, he slowly closed the wooden chest on his desk. Placing it alongside one of equal size, he clicked the lock into place and wiped the sweat off his forehead. Straightening his jacket with rigid wiping, he unlatched the catch and opened the door, inhaling the strong scent of the salt air whipping around the ship.

Standing a full head taller and sporting a robust and groomed beard, dressed in clothes no sailor could afford, locked a stare. Shrinking his character with piercing bright green eyes, nodding to the stern of the ship, he signaled Hugo to the observation deck. Greeting him with wide eyes and wet slicked-back hair, Hugo started to speak but was silenced by the raised hand of Verrazzano.

"Not much of size, but occupied; look at the number of fires," the captain pointed out over the dark water at the triangle-shaped island.

Sailing around toward a possible port, Verrazzano turned to stare as the island shrank on the horizon. "We'll baptize it in the illustrious name of our mother, Aloysia." The captain performed the act.

"Looks like it's just a little chip off the block, huh, captain?" Hugo stood awaiting orders.

"Ready the boats and prepare to drop anchors on my word, steer clear of that rough point over there." Verrazzano pointed, projecting his voice, asserting his command and position.

"Yes, skipper." Hugo turned around and barked orders for the rest of the crew of *The Dauphine*.

Verrazzano let a slight grin slip, watching Hugo, the mad-dog first mate, rip into everyone. He looked up at the sails. France's blue, white, and red flag flew at the highest point as the three-masted wooden carrack rode the tide toward the shore of an unknown coast. As the sun sank behind the cloud line on the horizon, he waited for the dark clouds to appear.

"Captain, captain, your presence is requested," the hail came through the thick oak door.

Verrazzano opened his eyes immediately and had one leg on the planking of the captain's cabin in a heartbeat. The motion was ingrained in his muscles from panic, fear, and excitement, or all three combined from the uncertainty starting each day of his journey.

Catching the graying of the morning sky out the stern windows while dressing, he racked his brain for where on Earth he was. A quick rap on the door followed by the muffled speech of multiple people quickened Verrazzano's pace. Opening the door with his knife behind his back, he calmed at the sight of Hugo, until the first mate started to speak.

"Morning, Captain, sorry to wake you at such a time."

"Don't worry your soul; an expedition such as ours calls for attentiveness and a quick heart to action." Verrazzano sheathed his knife and glanced over Hugo's shoulder, catching the subtle movement of a couple of seamen in the morning haze.

"Captain, we have a disciplinary action to invoke."

"What's the charge?"

"Benoit, the boatswain, was making his rounds below deck when he stumbled across a man with the name of Gaston; he was found with another man's belongings and assaulted Benoit when confronted."

Hugo watched the expression on Verrazzano's face drop to a wave of fierce, focused anger he had only witnessed once before.

The sun peeked over the edge of the ocean as seagulls circled overhead, cackling at each other, fighting over a quahog, while the crew surrounded the accused sailor, Gaston. Bound hands and feet, his face was already bruised from the punching he sustained on his climb up the ship's decks, already convicted by the crew through rumors and small talk. Hugo shook his head in disapproval as two men placed Gaston in front of him.

"What do you have to say for yourself? And might I add, mark your words carefully, for they can hold more weight than saying nothing at all," Hugo stated.

"I didn't take his goods. I was set up. Benny hates me," Gaston pleaded his hopeless case, seen guilty by every staring eyeball on deck.

"Nobody steals from Benny; that's just wrong, state the charges."

"Theft of Benny's goods and assault on a shipmate," Benoit shook his head in disgust.

"I saw 'im do it, ya thieving bastard," one man yelled out.

"I seen 'im take it too, and his food rations," another sailor threw out the damning remarks.

"What say you?" Hugo asked the accused.

"I want the captain to hear my case," Gaston pleaded as his captors pulled the ropes on his wrists upward behind his back, bending his joints unnaturally, "Ahhhhhhhhhhh," Gaston yelled out.

"I've heard all I need to hear; you speak a high lie." The whole crew turned around as Verrazzano appeared from the forecastle in the bow of the ship.

"Captain, I've been unjustly accused of this crime; please hear the truth." Gaston spun around so fast he ripped the rope out of the hands of his handlers.

"Your peers have judged you; now I will lay down my verdict, citing the Lord." Verrazzano made his way to the stern of the ship. "You are guilty of a traitorous act, which has no place upon this ship and must be dealt with to convey its severity. May God have justice on your soul." Verrazzano was as calm and relaxed as could be, stating the verdict.

"Yeeeeeeaeaaaaaaahhhhhhh," the crew cheered at the decision.

"Hang 'im on the mizzenmast!"

"Hoist 'im up the yardarm!!"

"Lashing with the cat, turn 'im into chowder!!!"

The threats of punishment grew louder until the plethora of ideas coalesced into a growing chant. The multitude of nautical tortures with the possibility of death resulting was shouted one over another with enthusiasm. Each one brought more terror into the eyes of Gaston as he looked for the captain, but the captain was gone. Scanning around, he just caught the headmaster's cabin door shut.

"Keel-haul, KEEL-haul, KEEL-haul, KEEL-HAUL," the crew shouted in unison until Hugo corralled the unruly sailors, calming them down.

"Under God and the power granted to me on this ship, we find the accused, Gaston of Normandy, guilty."

"Yeeeeaaahhhhhhh," the crew cheered, finally settling down, waiting for the sentence.

"And the sentence will be…three passes of…keel-hauling," Hugo said, grinning.

The crew exploded with cheers and excitement at the opportunity to keel-haul someone, unaware of the actual brutality. The anxious sailors prepared the lines to the yardarm for the torturous act.

Verrazzano, a profoundly religious man, wanted no part of the antics involved in the procedure. Locking his door and double-checking it, he stood in front of his chest at the end of the bed, keyed the lock, and lifted the leather-strapped lid. He removed the blankets, exposing the two small coffers at the bottom of the chest. Picking up the one on the right, which was lighter, he brought it to his desk, unlatched the clasp, and slowly lifted the top, staring at the item. He recited a prayer before reaching in and placing the other on his desk. While slowly examining the precious property, another cheer erupted outside his door on the ship's main deck. Verrazzano twitched at another chaotic outburst five minutes later and closed his eyes, blocking out the noise from outside, remembering when he first touched the ancient paradigm.

*June 10th, 1951*
*Prudence Island*

The end of the school year was approaching, and the twenty kids ran out of the one-room schoolhouse. With only half a dozen kids his age on the island, Thomas Blackburn had little chance of choosing his friends. Jason Walsh approached with his girlfriend. He was a year older, turning 14 in the winter. His girlfriend Kelly was naturally beautiful and already adored by all the boys of every age.

"Hey, Tommy," Jason yelled, trying to catch up to him.

"What's up, Jay?"

"Hey, I scored some smokes from my old man; you want to head to the cave and light 'em up?"

"I don't know, my parents are gonna smell it on me; I'll get the belt." Tommy kept walking down the gravel road as a car drove by, kicking up a wall of dust.

"Come on, Tommy, I got a couple of cherry bombs from my Uncle Greg," Kelly said, putting her arm around his shoulder. "Come on, it'll be fun; there's nothing else to do on this boring island anyway."

"Well, all right, but I gotta be home by five-thirty, or else I'll have my ass handed to me on a platter."

"Nice, cool, come on," Kelly said, walking backward down the road, blowing him a kiss and sending him into dreamland. "Follow me to the cave," she did her best creature feature voice.

They veered down an unused, overgrown road leading to the barren World War II Navy Depot base. Halfway to the base, they took a left down a ravine in the woods with a well-worn walking path made by generations of people drawn to the natural cave. Reaching the base of the wooded gully, they walked through the cave's entrance.

The narrow tunnel, barely six feet across, slowly widened to a cathedral rock shelter. A fire pit of loose stones against one wall was old but usable. An aperture created a natural draft that kept the chamber from filling up with smoke. Kelly had gathered some dead wood on the trip through the forest and started a small fire in the room, illuminating the aged carvings, paintings, and graffiti on the walls.

"Check it out: I snagged these Camels from my pops." Jason pulled out an Altoids tin and retrieved a couple of smokes. "Kelly, grab me a stick, would ya, sweetheart."

"Sure thing there, my main squeeze." She lit up her smoke, then held the match out.

"You want one, Tommy?"

"I don't know; I probably shouldn't."

"Come on; it's all right, just don't inhale too much. Watch." Jay took a long drag, showing him how, trying to look cool.

"Yeah, watch this." Kelly took a drag, blowing smoke rings, then exhaled the smoke out her nostrils like a dragon.

"All right, just one." Tommy caved in and coughed up a lung on his first hit, bringing Jay and Kelly to laughter.

"Cover your ears," Jay yelled as he lit one of the cherry bombs, throwing it on the other side of the cavern. The explosion shook them five times as much as it should have, reverberating around the rock walls.

"Wow, that was awesome," Tommy said, puffing away, thinking he was the coolest cat in the land.

"Got any more?" Jay asked Kelly.

"Yeah, hold on," Kelly replied, digging into her purse. "Got it."

"Nice, lemme see." Jay reached for it.

"I wanna light one, get outta here," Kelly said, cuddling the firecracker. Lighting the wick, she threw it, then waited for the sparks to stop. Suddenly, the whole cave started shaking.

The three friends all stared at each other with complete looks of panic. The entire cave was rocking, dropping pebbles, bouncing off the floor. Then bigger chunks of stone broked off the ceiling and smashed into the ground, breaking into smaller pieces.

The cherry bomb went off, sending Kelly screaming and causing a chain reaction of fear and terror. The Earth shook harder, dropping larger and larger slabs of stone. The kids looked at each other, then turned to the tunnel leading out. Jay bolted first, followed by the others. A boulder dropped in front of them, just a step away from the entrance. It caught Jay on the head, stunning and sending him stumbling back into the other two, while the Earth continued to shake and shatter.

The walls began to crack, sending sheared stone rumbling across the ground.

"We're going to die! Run! GO, RUN," Kelly screamed, standing up, pulling on the boys' shirts.

Turning around, she watched a fissure form above the entrance and slowly split the rock. A boulder smashed into the fire pit, sending burning embers into the air in all directions, darkening the cavern. Jay, still delirious, wiped the searing charcoal from his skin when two slabs of solid rock separated, falling to the ground, completely blocking the only way out of the cave.

After growing up in Italy, Verrazzano moved to France. He considered himself a Florentine, and returned to Italy by request from the pope upon hearing of his granted exploration across the ocean. Accepting the invitation to the Vatican, Verrazzano stayed there for a month, learning of his true purpose on the voyage.

He accepted the ancient relics and his underlying mission and returned to France to prepare his ships for the biggest adventure of his life, which held a more profound meaning with a more significant purpose than his primary objectives. The precious items in his chest were always guarded until he embarked on the most infamous Atlantic crossing in history. Tragedy struck a week out, sinking all boats in the exploratory flotilla except Verrazzano's flagship, *The Dauphine*.

Seeking refuge in the Azores, Verrazzano took it as a sign from the heavens to continue his unique journey alone, not wanting any interference or distraction from disturbed minds, who might inquire about the underlying motives. The crew was of pleasant spirits through a month of good sailing and decent weather days. Sailing across the vastest section of the Atlantic Ocean, they headed toward the unknown, having no record of any explorer finding land at this latitude.

The winds died down to a baby's breath as *The Dauphine* rocked on the ocean swells, and the crew started to mumble. After two days of minuscule wind, even Hugo, the first mate, was agitated.

Hugo knocked on the door twice and took off his hat, waiting for the skipper's presence. "Captain, could I have a word please."

The door opened and a stern-faced Verrazzano stood rigid. "Hugo, come inside, please. What is that crawling on the floor?" He closed the door and locked it.

"A big bug, it looks blue," Hugo said, stepping on it and squashing it into the floorboards. The concerned look on Hugo's face portrayed what Verrazzano already knew: an idle boat in the middle of the ocean can lead to thoughts of despair, fear, panic, and mutiny. The calm demeanor of the captain put Hugo at ease, which he hoped would transfer throughout the crew.

"Splice the main brace twice," Verrazzano stated, and allowed double portions of grog, which might be a blessing or a curse; time would tell.

Once Hugo left, Verrazzano locked his door, checked it twice, and produced the two coffers, opening them on his desk. Pulling out the contents of both boxes, then laying them out on the folded cloth in which they were wrapped, he thought about what he was doing and the words of Pope Clement VII:

"Be careful of the words for if used correctly in unison with the Earthly spectrum stones, unnatural power can be obtained using ancient and forgotten channels, abandoned and buried by the church as blasphemy. You might discover the origin of these on your journey and possibly find a profound use, even more powerful than we can imagine. These usages do come with a warning, for every use tips you toward a terrible fate. Anyone who has tempted this curse to gain power has come to a horrible ending. Do not fret, my son, if you find the necessity to delve; these tales are ancient. If your motives are pure, the severity will be lessened. The origins of these relics are said to arise from Atlantis, sent out on a ship during the supposed destruction of the great ringed city. Greek sailors found an abandoned boat filled with skeletal remains with one clutching to the boxes you now hold." The pope intertwined his fingers and stared into Verrazzano's eyes.

Beholding the contents of the ancient artifacts, Verrazzano decided to partake in the almost extinct ritual given to him. Different levels of severity could be attained with different combinations between the two coffers. Verrazzano was desperate for wind and summoned the ancient words as he held the archaic crystals in his hand.

Hours passed, but nothing happened. He decided to step out on the observation deck for fresh air.

Two steps up, the mainsail started flapping for the first time in days.

*It worked,* he told himself, shaking it off as dumb luck; *The wind could have kicked up naturally without any help,* he thought.

A more significant gust came, filling all the sails, lurching the ship forward, and continued for two days. Bringing joy and positive energy, the vessel gained much-needed distance when, on the third day, the wind ceased and didn't return for another two, placing him in the same situation as before, stranded in the middle of the Atlantic Ocean with fifty men.

Convinced of the atavistic measures taken before, he locked himself in his cabin. Verrazzano decided to up the ante and quadruple the power of the formula holding four different crystals and stones in his hand, and he recited the venerable words.

Feeling the crystals heat up in his hands, he watched sparks seem to bounce around inside of the different colored stones as he recited the words. As the stones reached a temperature hot enough to burn his skin, he finished the phrasing in its entirety, then dropped the time-worn earth rocks onto his desk. He examined his hand.

As he wrapped the stones in the cloth, he could still feel the heat emanating. His skin was swelling, and he quickly packed up the items into the coffers. Now feeling guilty for practicing what would be considered black magic, he locked the contents in his chest and prayed every prayer he knew, begging forgiveness for not having faith in God to bring wind. Verrazzano perceived that he had touched the devil from the burn, and he called his cabin boy to fetch a pail of seawater, which he blessed as he submerged his hand, instantly feeling relief from the cold ocean. He held it there until the stinging stopped. Afraid to look at his hand, fearing he'd been marked by evil, he ran ideas through his head to explain his injury.

Once again, Verrazzano made his way to the observation deck after returning his cabin to normalcy. Hugo approached and looked at the bandage around the captain's hand, but didn't ask.

Still, Verrazzano answered anyway. "Spilled the pool of wax on my hand from the big candle on my desk. Burns like hell," he added, noting the irony and guilt in his head.

Without a trace of wind for hours, he was convinced the first time was a fluke. *But what of my hand? What was that?* he thought, when a proud gust caught the crew and Verrazzano unawares, filling the sails with such force the ship listed to portside, sending all of them off their feet, scrambling for balance.

"Captain, look," Hugo shouted, holding onto the top rail and pointing out over the ocean. The beautiful clear blue sky showed a wall of white rain approaching, encompassed with black billowing clouds, slowly filling the sky to the south and creeping fast.

The swells reached the boat well before the storm, rocking it to the point of capsizing. Stripping the masts bare, they rode out the hurricane for what seemed like forever. Immeasurable gusts of wind threatened to tip the ship and would toss anyone stupid enough to venture above deck into the ocean without any hope of recovery. Riding out the storm with the cabin boy and Hugo, Verrazzano thought he had doomed the ship and killed them all. He prayed constantly for safety as the wooden boat creaked with every impact.

As the ship's crew was bailed water at a rate that couldn't keep up with the constant flow every time the vessel was smashed with breaking waves, everything just stopped, and the seas leveled out. The crew under the deck was unsure if they had sunk deeper into the ocean because of the stillness. Verrazzano thought the same until a beam of sunlight streamed through the stern windows of the captain's cabin.

Hugo ventured out onto the deck first and confirmed they were in the clear. He called the crew up and, opening all the doors and hatches, screamed his usual orders. The wind was steady and continued to drive them across the ocean until they found seabirds. They landed on the outer banks of what is now North Carolina a month and a half later, completing the longest route across the Atlantic Ocean.

The persistent, black-clouded front approached again, and they dropped multiple anchors, riding out the storm. They popped anchors from the swell and wind combinations, causing Verrazzano once again to pray, to ask forgiveness for using the black magic to call upon the 'Devil's Wind.' Bouncing their way up the unmapped coast of North America, they anchored at the mouth of the Hudson River and sent forward the boats to explore farther north. After a lull in the storm, Verrazzano decided to sail east, attempting to outrun the wind and tidal surge. Days later, he approached the triangle-shaped island. Anchoring off the coast, he was awakened by a knock, with Hugo asking him to sentence the thief.

Removing himself from the keel-haul verdict, Verrazzano stared at the chest on his desk once again. He wondered if he should just throw them out the window, remembering the pope's warning.

Verrazzano questioned the misfortune of his decision. *Is the curse on me or the ship? Will the calamity stay with us or stay with the chests?*

As he risked bringing the ship closer to shore, natives came out in their hollowed-out canoes, greeting them cheerfully and offering items to trade. Another front could be seen building up and approaching fast. Verrazzano feared this would be the one that would cause the sinking of *The Dauphine*, ending his mission, but the natives guided them through a break in the land to the new port. The captain and crew were shocked as the clouds cleared to a beautiful bay.

Precisely shown the way, Verrazzano and Hugo were in awe as they s-turned through a passage and anchored in a completely protected harbor. They imagined they had obtained God's providence. Safe on all sides from the ocean and tucked in the bottom of a valley against the wind, they couldn't believe their luck or their eyes.

The storm raged for three days, rocking the ship, but was minimal in their newfound harbor, which Verrazzano named Refuge. The decision was made to replenish their provisions and socialize with the natives and learn their customs. Meeting the two kings, Miantonomo and Conanicus, Verrazzano found them the most elegant and decorated natives of all they came across in the new land. They were invited to the village, and Verrazzano and his crew became the first Europeans to set foot on the ground, later discovering it was an island and named it Rhodes because of the resemblance to the isle of Rhodes in the Mediterranean. Thinking he beat the 'devil's wind,' Verrazzano explored the bay over the next week, mapping out the various rocky points carefully, but cut his trip short when the sky turned black once more. They buckled down in the harbor for another week.

Thinking the storm might follow him forever, Verrazzano met with Hugo and discussed his contrived plan during the storm. Hugo set out into the bay with three boats during the witch's hour. He returned to *The Dauphine* with two, accomplishing his mission.

*June 1951*
*Prudence Island*

The rumbling stopped, and the cave was pitch black, except for a sliver of natural light from the entrance and a plenitude splattering of orange coals from the fire. Pebbles continued to bounce off the ground, creating the only sound in the deafening silence.

"We're trapped in here," Kelly said shakily. "Jay? Tommy?"

"Yeah, I'm here. I got clocked on the head," Jay said, gingerly touching the ever-swelling knot on his head.

"I think it was an earthquake," Tommy concluded.

"In Rhode Island? No way, that's a California thing," Kelly said.

"It was definitely an earthquake," Jay agreed, standing up. "Or the Russians just bombed us."

"What are we gonna do?" Kelly said with a growing worry in her voice.

After removing the boulder from the fire pit, they struck up another blaze with some matches and quickly assessed that they were trapped in the cave. They cried and yelled for help until their throats felt like razor blades. Not giving up, Tommy explored every nook and cranny of the cave.

"We're gonna die in here," Kelly kept saying, sounding hopeless, as Jay held his arm around her.

"Hey guys, come here, check it out," Tommy called them over.

"What is it?" Jay stoked the fire, offering more light.

"I don't know." Tommy worked his hands into a crevice, seeming to move a boulder by himself until it came crashing to the ground.

"Holy smokes," Jay said, and helped move another giant stone. "This might be another way out."

Without much effort, one rock gave way to another, and the boys removed dozens, sending them crumbling down as if someone had stacked them up on top of the boulder unseen until the earthquake shook them loose, making them visible.

"What do you see?" Jay asked Tommy, who had crawled up on the boulder and disappeared into the rock. "Hey, Tommy, where'd ya go?"

"Tommy," Kelly echoed, concerned.

"Tommy, you all right, man? Hey, answer, you're freaking us out," Jay started climbing. "Whoa."

"What is it?" Kelly asked, the only one left in the cave as Jay disappeared over the boulder.

"Wow," Jay said. He handed his makeshift torch to Tommy, then ripped his shirt up to feed the fire.

A secondary cavern, slightly smaller than the main chamber, was flooded with light from the torch.

"Maybe this is another way out," Tommy said with enthusiasm that was quickly dashed, as he explored the walls and found no other outlet. "What the hell."

"No luck," came a voice behind them, scaring them until they turned and saw Kelly's face. "What's that over there?"

"I don't know," Tommy said. "There's writing above it."

He reached for a bundle of old blankets in a rock niche in the cave wall. He picked up the fabric; it was fragile to the touch. "There's a name on it," he said. Tommy exposed a small chest covered with cracked animal skin. "It says 'Giovanni da Verrazzano,' who's that? And why is this in here?"

"I read about him; he was an explorer in Columbus's time. He got captured by native cannibals in the Caribbean, cooked alive, and eaten in front of his crew," Kelly said seriously.

"Is that true? Jesus, that's awful, awful bad luck. Open it, maybe it's his treasure." Jay was excited, and held the lit torch over the chest.

"Yeah, we'll be rich, with no way to spend it unless we get out of this death hole," Kelly said, anxiously awaiting the contents.

Tommy slowly opened the box and saw another sheaf of some sort of fabric. He pulled the object out of the coffer and peeled back the covering, as they all stood and stared at the artifact.

"What in the….."

"You gotta be kiddin' me."

"Wow," Tommy said, touching the primordial book of Atlantis bound in ancient animal hide. There were thick pages of a similar make.

"A book?" Kelly said, disappointed.

"No gold or treasure?" Jay said, equally let down.

"This is awesome." Tommy flipped through the pages, some of which contained petrified pressed flowers and feathers from a time long gone.

"What language is that?" Kelly asked, looking at the strange combination of shapes, letters, and lines, looking like a cross between every cultural writing in one.

"I don't know. I've never seen anything like this, but underneath each line is Latin. I know that for sure. It's like somebody translated the lines into Latin. I think it's a sorcerer's book or something." Tommy was enthralled.

"Hey, there's more," Jay said, holding the light in the nook. "Look."

Jay lifted the second item, struggling as it was much heavier than he anticipated. He pulled it toward himself and leaned into the nook to support the weight. A ratcheting sound clicked, causing him to pause his movement.

"Jay, drop it," Tommy yelled out a second too late.

A weighted blade came slicing down, severing both of Jay's hands off at the wrist. It sent the second chest rolling out of its fabric covering, spilling its contents along with Jay's separated hands as he fell backward in shock.

Atlantian crystals and stones of every make and color, gathered from around the continents in ancient times and passed down through generations, of immeasurable worth and power if used correctly, scattered across the ground next to the book.

Kelly and Tommy looked at the irreplaceable treasure, then at Jay, who was in shock and panic. He stared at his missing hands as blood began to surge.

"What are we going to do?" Kelly looked at Tommy, white in the face.

Tommy looked from Jay to the book to Kelly. "Can you read Latin?"

ଔ

Growing up in the East Bay of Rhode Island, **Pete Rock** is a musician and writer who pulls inspiration from all walks of life, great and terrible. He lives with his wife, Sarah, on Aquidneck Island and enjoys long walks along the beach during hurricanes.

# Carefree

*by Jess M. Collette*

*S*ail away on the Block Island Ferry, take a trip back to
*carefree times.* It's catchy. That's why Cora can't stop
hearing it. The jingle is stuck in her head, and she's stuck
in the minivan with her mom, dad, and younger brother Paul. As the
song suggests, they're all about to sail away on the Block Island
ferry. Her dad's driving them to their annual summer getaway, and
much to Cora's chagrin, he's singing the song as he steers. Behind
him in the back seat, she's slouching and refuses to participate. Despite her embarrassment, her family sings loudly. Their voices are
robust enough to fill the van and spill out through the open windows.
Curious looks from people in vehicles nearby prove just how far
their voices travel. Cora dips a bit lower in her seat.

This famous song has never resonated with her during her
almost 18 years of family vacations to "The Block." She looks at the
smiling eyes of the others as they sing. Her mom, dad, and Paul seem
to grasp its vibe completely. Each of them can transfer to island time
without a second thought. She would be the first to admit that she
has always been a little more tightly wound than the rest of them.
Cora has always found it hard to relax, even when she was younger.
Now, it's no different and maybe even harder. It has only gotten
worse since she is coming off the most stressful time of her life –
her senior year of high school.

Sure, she thought graduation would have been a huge stress
reliever, but it only reminded her that college was no more than a
couple of months away. The last four years of high school had been
something. Something she struggled to describe. Those years had
been a crazy dance of fitting in and standing out, being good, but not
being *too good*, and finding first love while learning to gracefully –

or sometimes not so gracefully – let it go. High school was heavy. Cora's shoulder began to ache as she let her thoughts drift back to the days she had just left behind. Her fingers massaged the ridge her bookbag had eroded into her shoulder over those tumultuous years. Like the mishmash of emotions she carried, she hoped the intensity of that ache would also fade with time.

Dad's abrupt turn and too fast approach to a well-placed speed bump shook Cora from her worries and threatened to launch her six-year-old brother from his booster seat. The quick catch from his seatbelt clicked and locked. It kept Paul from going airborne, but Jeff, her brother's beloved goldfish, sloshed precariously in the water bag Paul grasped. Cora watched her younger brother readjust in his seat before leaning down and asking Jeff if he was okay. Paul took a sip from a green-and-white-striped cup before puckering his lips and placing a Del's frozen lemonade-coated kiss on the clear plastic bag that separated the boy from the fish.

Cora couldn't help but find it cute that her brother's strawberry-blond hair was a close color match to Jeff, the goldfish's warm golden glow. She noticed Jeff seemed a little off-kilter, and as she looked closer, saw that his dorsal fin drooped to the right. Maybe he was fighting a touch of seasickness. If that was even possible for a fish, she didn't know, but she sure knew it was possible for her. On more than one occasion, Cora had fought a stomach-churning battle with seasickness on the ferry. She takes a sip from her water bottle, swallows hard, and hopes today's trip will be smoother.

After a few forwards and reversals that displace some seagulls from picking up scattered potato chips on the lot, her dad finally fits the minivan into a tight parking spot in the first row. The seagulls glare down on the van from their perches on the shipyard moorings. As her mom flings her door wide, followed by her dad's and then Paul's, Cora can hear the displeased squawks multiply, and the flap of wings intensify as the hungry birds take flight and hover above. Her mom waves her oversized beach hat in the air, shooing them before turning her attention to the luggage in the back hatch.

Cora isn't moving. She knows she has a few minutes to spare while her mom double-checks everything. She is preoccupied in the back seat, staring at her reflection in the rearview mirror. She pushes in with her fingers on the slight puffiness she sees beneath her eyes. She looks tired. She is tired. Right now, all she can attempt to decide is if her ponytail should be high, low, or side. She pulls the elastic from around her wrist and flips her head between her knees. In one fluid movement, she's sitting upright, with a high pony secured in place. The hatch beeps as it closes, alerting Cora. It's time for her to move.

She joins her family behind the crowd that shuffles slowly toward and onto the boat. Some drag luggage, roll bikes, and lead dogs. Only one carries a goldfish. Walking behind them, Cora can't help but sympathize with Jeff. As she watches the little golden fish slosh about in the plastic bag in her brother's hand, she also feels unprepared for what is ahead. At this point, Cora is also merely along for the ride. She puts one foot in front of the other and notices she is wearing different colored flip-flops, navy and black. She hopes the close colors aren't apparent to others, but she knows the bright sunshine exposes everything. The glare from the sun off her dad's super-white knee-high socks he's wearing with shorts reminds her of that. She repeatedly blinks from the sun-blindness. White knee-high socks with shorts! She figures maybe mismatched flip-flops aren't so bad.

She follows her parents as they make their way through the congregating people to find their usual spot in the front of the ferry. The headwind is strong, and the boat isn't even moving yet. The gusts quickly grab onto Cora's high ponytail and whip it around. Round and round, it spins. Cora waves her hands to get her parents' attention before pointing her finger down to indicate that she will be going to her preferred seat on the lower level of the boat. Her dad waves, and her mom blows her a kiss. Cora makes her way back through the crowd to where she knows she'll find her quiet spot. She knows from experience that she will also have a better chance of avoiding seasickness downstairs.

Cora adjusts her wind-loosened ponytail as she settles into her seat at the back of the boat. She notices an elderly couple sitting across from her with a Chihuahua between them. They take turns feeding/patting, patting/feeding the little dog. All look happy and content. She wouldn't mind trading places with any of them. She runs her hands down her long dark blonde hair, smoothing the strands that the ocean wind had disheveled. Some spring back, defiantly empowered by the salty air.

She slowly takes a deep breath and applies gloss to her windblown lips. The ferry engines fire and the PA system crackles before the captain announces the boat's departure. What she needs now is music. She places her earbuds in and selects her "chill" playlist, which consists of various tunes from the 70s. Though that era was way before her time, its classic music somehow moves her and calms her soul. After observing a few more rounds of feeding/patting and patting/feeding the Chihuahua, Cora turns to watch the frothy water retreat behind the boat.

The boat sways but not too much; it seems in time with the music. Cora's worries shift as she watches the mainland harbor get smaller. "Summer Breeze" plays through her earbuds as the summer breeze ripples across her cotton tank top. The ocean air tickles the skin on her shoulders ever so slightly, leaving a path of raised hairs to show where it has been. She removes the elastic holding her ponytail in place and watches the invisible force of the wind scatter her hair. She sees him as she turns her head to tame the wild strands with her fingers.

He's leaning on the railing across from her, just visible behind the couple with the Chihuahua. How had she missed him before? His summer-colored curls bounce perfectly with the motion of the waves. He has an effortless tan that seamlessly covers his face to his feet. Of course, unlike her, he is wearing matching flip-flops, navy blue, on both feet. Cora immediately feels uncomfortable and slides her mismatched flip-flops farther beneath the bench where she sits. They hide in the shadow below. She looks back toward him, and though he is wearing sunglasses, she feels his eyes upon her. Cora immediately shifts her gaze. She fiddles with her earbuds, examining one in her hand when two perfectly tanned feet wearing blue flip-flops step into view.

"Seat taken?" His voice matches his look, laid-back yet assertive.

"No. Yes. I mean, you can sit here," Cora responds.

He runs his fingers through his curls, with one side of his mouth upturned, exposing a cheek dimple on the same side. "Listening to anything good?"

Cora looks at the earbud in her hand and then quickly removes the remaining one from her ear. She ponders whether to tell him the truth about what music she is listening to, and then she doesn't think and speaks. "'Summer Breeze,'" Cora says as more of a question than a statement.

"You probably don't know it," she says as she fiddles with her earbud. "It's a song from a long time ago."

"Seals and Crofts," he says without pause.

Cora studies him, her eyes wide as she wonders if he had somehow read the playlist on her phone.

"I get it," he says in response to her puzzled expression, "most kids our age don't know that music. But for me, I'm a west coast boy, and I love its relaxed vibe." He leans back and stretches his legs out straight. "Always have, always will."

Cora pauses to see if she believes what she is hearing. She decides she does. "I'm Cora, born and raised in Rhode Island."

"Ethan. Born and raised in California. I'm visiting my grandparents on Block Island." He waits for a beat and then adds, "I guess I'm an old soul, as are you, it appears."

Cora and Ethan's banter is non-stop while on the Block Island ferry. They agree life isn't much different on the west coast as it is on the east coast; good music is good music, fried fish tastes good tucked in a taco or served on a plate with chips, and chance encounters between east- and west-coasters can happen if you're willing to take a chance. Ethan also reveals that though he is apprehensive about college, he is also excited.

"A new start shouldn't scare us," he says with his arms held wide. "It should revive us. As we've heard them say, the world is our oyster, and I believe that. I believe that sometimes you'll find a pearl when you're not even looking for one."

Ethan reaches toward Cora. "Can I get that?" She shakes her head yes. He gently picks up a few strands of her hair that had blown and stuck to her lip gloss. As he tucks them behind her ear, she smiles and blushes. She wonders if he notices the warmth flooding into her cheeks. She shyly looks away. As her eyes peer down, she doesn't see her mismatched flip-flops, she feels no signs of seasickness, and she is entirely unaware the couple with the Chihuahua are now admiring her and Ethan.

The ferry PA system crackles, and the captain's voice says they are soon arriving at their destination, Block Island. Cora has never had a ferry ride go by so fast. For once, she doesn't want it to end. *Sail away on the Block Island ferry, take a trip back to carefree times.* The jingle she could not get out of her head earlier now reaches Cora and Ethan, where they sit. She knows immediately from where it has originated. Over the years, she had seen her dad in the front of the boat singing the jingle alone for a moment until, like waves, it spread around the ship and returned to him where it started, a whole chorus of ferry passengers strong.

Cora sings so the jingle will return to her dad. Cora sings for herself. She turns toward Ethan and raises her eyes to see her bright reflection in his blue mirrored sunglasses. The wind encourages her hair to dance as the sun's rays kiss away the dullness. Her reflection shows an easy smile, not forced or for show. It matches the contentment she feels deep inside. It is apparent that this is a moment. It has never been more evident that this is a time to which she will want to take a trip back. It is her reflection in his sunglasses that she never wants to unsee. She stares a bit longer, capturing it. Carefree looks good on her.

ભ

**Jess M. Collette** has always called New England home. She has lived in Massachusetts, Vermont, and Rhode Island. The beauty and ever-changing seasons in this region inspire her writing. In addition to nature, Jess also writes about love and loss, drawing from her own experience of losing her only child, Joshua. In his honor, she has published two books. In addition to writing, she also makes unique creations with graphic design. Jessica lives in Rhode Island with her husband and their adorable rescue dog from Texas. Visit www.jessicamcollette.com for updates and to view current writing, poetry, and designs.

# The Summer Secret

*by Brielle Lilygarten*

The sweat dripped down the back of my neck. The whir of the beach bus engine started, and it lurched forward. It was packed with mostly teenagers after a long, hot day at Scarborough Beach. I had just finished my shift at Iggy's and could feel my feet throbbing from standing all day. I sat back and slowly chewed my doughboy as I thought about the events of the day. The sugar crystals melted on my tongue, and I swished them down with my soda.

My mind flashed back to the beginning of the summer when I first got hired at Iggy's. I knew it would be filled with a lot of fun and entertainment, and a lot of hard work. It was the summer before my junior year, so I wanted it to be a good one filled with sun, sand, and fun with friends. I couldn't think of a more perfect job. My best friend, Shaina, and I got hired together, so I just knew the summer was going to be great.

What I didn't expect was to fail my driving test. *Isla, you didn't use your blinker when you turned. Automatic fail.* That sentence kept echoing in my head. I had pictured Shaina and me driving to work, windows down, music blasting, hair blowing in the wind. Instead, I was stuck on the awful beach bus, sweating and miserable. I closed my eyes and listened to the hum and chatter.

I woke up the next day and started getting ready for my shift, when I got a call from my manager at Iggy's. I needed to report to work immediately. The lines were already down the sidewalk and the staff couldn't handle the crowd. I threw on my uniform, checked the bus schedule, and headed out to the bus stop. The sun was already beating down on me and it was only 9:00 am. I knew it was going to be another hot one.

I walked into Iggy's and felt the hot air smack me in the face. One downfall about working there in the summer was there was no AC. I tied up my hair, put on a smile, and got ready to serve my first of many customers of the day. It was only a month into the summer, but already I was familiar with the regulars. We had several customers who visited us weekly, some even daily. It was nice to see the familiar faces, strike up some small chit-chat, and hear about their summer adventures.

One customer in particular always caught my eye. He kept to himself and ordered the same thing – a half dozen doughboys and a soda. He would take his order and sit quietly on one of the benches overlooking the ocean, sometimes sitting for an hour or two. I was curious about him, especially because he always came alone and seemed to have all the time in the world to just sit and take in his surroundings. He wore a wedding ring, so I assumed his significant other had passed. No one ever really said anything about him, just "oh, there's Mr. Worthen again, such a sweet guy." All of the staff loved waiting on him, and he was equally happy to see everyone.

"Order number 167, 168, 169, 170…your orders are ready!" yelled Marco from behind the counter.

"Julissa, come on, we need more napkins!"

"Sam, grab one more water and a pack of ketchup for order number 168," barked Marco.

People rushed the counter and snapped me out of my thoughts. I knew I needed to get my head in the game and start hustling. I pushed my own worries and woes out of my mind and got right to work. I stuffed napkins, forks, and ketchup packets into the bags and handed them to the eager customers awaiting their food. A young mother with two children dropped half of the order and we needed a rush on two hamburgers and chicken tenders. She grimaced in embarrassment as the youngest child started crying. *Only five more hours until my shift is over*, I thought.

The rest of the day was filled with a hectic blur of orders coming up, customers pushing their way to the front of the line so they could try to get their food more quickly, and the hot, stifling air whirring around in the restaurant from the overhead fans. I took a moment to breathe and looked up at the clock. The day had flown by, and I only had 15 more minutes until the end of my shift.

When the clock struck three, I grabbed my bag and flew out the door. I had 45 minutes until the next bus, so I decided to take a walk down by the water. The sun was still beating down strong, and I felt beads of sweat trickle down my neck. I walked along the water and dipped my feet into the ocean. As I walked, I noticed Mr. Worthen sitting on his park bench, watching the waves. I held up my hand to wave and he waved back. I don't know what it was that day that made me want to strike up a conversation with him, but I decided to walk over to his bench and say hello.

"Hi, Mr. Worthen. Enjoying the waves?" I asked.

"I love sitting here, watching the waves. It is so peaceful, and I can get lost in my thoughts very easily. It brings me back to a much simpler, happier time, and I love reminiscing about my days here," he replied.

We sat next to each other for a while in silence. I thought about striking up a conversation several times, but for some reason, chose to enjoy the silence and peacefulness between us.

"Well." I stood up, almost too abruptly. "I've got to catch my bus. I'll be seeing you soon."

"Yep, see you soon," replied Mr. Worthen.

I picked up my bag and rushed off to the bus stop. I couldn't stop thinking about Mr. Worthen the whole way home.

Weeks passed with the same mundane routine. The summer I had pictured wasn't turning out to be what was happening. Ride the beach bus to work. Work my shift at Iggy's. Ride the beach bus back home. *Blah*. Sure, I got to hang out with my friends, spend days at the beach, and enjoy some downtime, but it just wasn't the same without being able to drive.

On Thursday morning, I arrived at work ten minutes before my shift began. I was opening and, unfortunately, my coworker had called out, so I had to open by myself. I walked around the back of the building to unlock the back door and screamed in surprise.

"AHHHHHH!" I screamed and all the keys and trays I was holding crashed to the ground.

"Sorry about that. I didn't mean to scare you."

"But wh-what are you doing here? We're not even open yet. Why are you hanging out by the back door?"

Mr. Worthen took a step back and sighed.

"I'm sorry, Isla. I thought I dropped my keys here and was just looking for them. I guess I'll be going now."

He hurried off and left me standing there dumbfounded. I opened the door and the Iggy's sign clanged, making me jump. I was still shaken by my encounter with Mr. Worthen. I tried to shake the feeling and continued opening the restaurant. My manager arrived and the day began with the hustle and bustle. I tried to forget about Mr. Worthen. I felt as though I should tell someone but didn't know who. Everyone loved Mr. Worthen and I doubted they would believe me.

A week later, I showed up to open and the police were there.

"Hello, miss, we were called to this location because someone saw a man trying to enter the back door."

My mind raced. It must have been Mr. Worthen again. What the heck was going on!

"Well, we don't see anything suspicious around here, but if you notice anything out of the ordinary, please give us a call. We're happy to check it out."

I thanked the police officer and opened the door to start the shift. I knew I should start getting ready for my shift, but could not help but wonder what Mr. Worthen was looking for. I was lost in thought when my manager interrupted me.

"Isla," yelled Marco. "What is your deal? Let's go. We need to get the burgers on the grill and the dough in the fryer."

I snapped to it and quickly got to work. I was still preoccupied by what had happened with Mr. Worthen but tried to push it out of my mind. I ran to the meat freezer to grab more burgers, and almost slipped on a piece of paper.

"What the—" I exclaimed. I bent down to pick up the paper. It took me a moment to realize it wasn't just a piece of paper. It was an old black-and-white photo of a young man. The face looked familiar, but I couldn't put my finger on it. I stuffed the photo into my back pocket and rushed back to the front of the restaurant.

Marco and I worked side by side in silence, prepping all the food before we opened.

I slowly prepared the fryer for the doughboys.

"Marco, what do you know about Mr. Worthen?"

"Not much. Why? He likes to hang around here. Kind of a lost soul. Quiet. Keeps to himself."

"I don't know. I just feel bad for him." I sighed.

My shift went by quickly despite all that was weighing on my mind. Five o'clock hit and I packed up, ready to catch the bus. I headed out to my favorite bench to wait and saw exactly who I was hoping would be there.

I plopped down on the bench. "Hi, Mr. Worthen. Hey, do you know who this is?" I whipped the photo out of my back pocket.

"My, my photo! Where did you find that?" Mr. Worthen exclaimed. "That's why I've been lurking around lately. That picture has more meaning to me than you could ever imagine. The day that picture was taken is ingrained my brain forever. It was one of the happiest days of my life. The day I opened my own business. Iggy's."

I sat there dumfounded. "You're the original owner of Iggy's? Does anyone even know that? Is that why you're always hanging around?" A million questions ran through my mind.

Mr. Worthen sighed. "Yes. This place has been my life and I have never wanted to let it go. I was never one for the fame. I preferred to be in the background making things happen, rather than taking the credit for the success. I love watching the hustle and bustle goes on every day and know that Iggy's still brings joy and happiness to so many people."

I stared at the photo. I knew why the face was so familiar. There was that same twinkle in the eyes. "Here, this means more to you than anyone." I pressed the photo into Mr. Worthen's hands and wrapped them around the photo. The bus screeched to a halt in front of the bus stop. I stood with a smile and boarded the bus. I rode the bus home in silence, thinking about Mr. Worthen, his story, and the realization that no matter how bad things might seem, there is always good in every situation.

ः

*This is a work of fiction. The original Iggy's doughboy shack in Oakland Beach (Warwick), Rhode Island, was started by Gaetano Gravino, who, with his wife Sally, established Iggy's Doughboy and Chowder House in 1989. The Iggy's name comes from a nickname Gaetano's son David bestowed upon him.*

**Brielle Lilygarten** is a veteran English teacher who has loved to read and write ever since she was a young girl. She published her first children's book, *Fishy, Fishy* in 2021 and is currently working on her second book. When Brielle is not reading or writing, she can be found spending time with her family, enjoying the outdoors, or trying to catch up on her never-ending to-do list. She is excited and honored to be featured in this year's Association of Rhode Island Authors Anthology. You can follow her on Instagram @brililybooks or check out her website at www.brililybooks.com.

# Rhode Island Summer Generations

*By Debbie Kaiman Tillinghast*

We pay our toll on the Mount Hope Bridge, summer has begun.
School vacation opens, with a day in the Newport sun.
We park our car in wispy grass, alongside Second Beach,
Then gaze across the soft white sand, as far as sight can reach.

We grab our towels from the car, and a jug of lemonade,
A cooler filled with sandwiches, the ones my mom has made.
Endless foam-topped swells roll in, upon the tidal rush,
We spread two blankets on the sand, and baby oil on us.

We top our curly hair with bright flowered bathing caps,
And squeal when any icy wave hits us with a smack.
Our bodies work as surfboards, we swim till time for lunch.
Then eat our tuna sandwiches, pickles add a crunch.

We rest for one whole hour, swim until we have to go,
Our faces now shine lobster red, and warm from the sun's glow.
We head home with one last stop, at Newport Creamery,
An ice cream cone to end our day, I choose strawberry.

Flash forward twenty-five years ahead,
We drive to Scarborough Beach instead.
Three boys, three girls, and two busy moms,
Head to the shore with much aplomb.

175

# Iconic Rhode Island

The oldest three line the wide back seat,
They hold three more, with dangling feet.
Pack towels, drinks, and a yummy lunch,
Bring along snacks for the kids to munch.

Since they have grown past baby stage,
We skip Sand Hill Cove to find bigger waves.
First spread sunscreen with a generous hand,
Then dive into the surf, or stretch on the sand.

The youngest two build fine castles tall,
Two moms sit and watch over them all.
They chat and laugh but don't look away,
Their eyes never leave their children at play.
As an orange sun slides into the sea,
We gather the blankets and shake the sand free.
On the way home, we all vote to stop,
Oatley's for ice cream will make our day tops.

I order Grape-Nut, a Rhode Island treat,
Return to the car, our excursion complete.
Two tired moms still ride home with big smiles,
Six sleepy children take naps all the while.

Flash forward once more, another thirty-five years,
When five grandchildren arrive with loud, joyful cheers.
They've packed towels, and shovels, and also their pails,
Brought one boogie board, across the shallows to sail.

Roger Wheeler State Beach earns our choice for safe play,
Now grandchildren's giggles swell my heart and the day.

They fill buckets with shells, to take home on the plane,
Add a collection of rocks, to paint if it rains.

When they tire of digging in the coarse, crusty sand,
We explore and find swings, but we keep holding hands.
I give each one a push, and make each one fly high,
Then they soar on the swings like the gulls in the sky.

Our trip ends with a taste that cannot be beat,
We stop by at Brickley's for ice cream cones sweet.
It will always hold true, though so many years pass,
Summer days at the beach create memories that last.

ߙ

**Debbie Kaiman Tillinghast** is the author of two books—*The Ferry Home,* a memoir about her childhood on Prudence Island, Rhode Island, and a novel, *A Dream Worth Keeping,* the story of one woman's journey to discover who she really is after a painful divorce.

Her writing has appeared in *Country* magazine, and her poetry has been featured in six anthologies published by the Association of Rhode Island Authors. Debbie is a retired teacher, and Nutrition Educator.

Visit her at www.debbiekaimantillinghast.com

# The Train of Thought Sometimes Takes the Road

*by Kevin Duarte*

**M**ore specifically, the East Bay bike path.

This pedestrian roadway, which stretches 15 miles along the Rhode Island coastline, experienced a metamorphosis several years ago. Originally the Providence and Bristol Railroad, its tracks were converted to the bike path soon after I graduated from Roger Williams University. The timing of this renovation was very convenient for me when, after moving from Bristol to Riverside - with a one-year layover in Warren - biking on the newly constructed path became my mode of transportation when I returned to the university as an employee a few years after I graduated.

Now on to my second job since leaving RWU six years ago, I had a sudden need to experience this commute again, fully focused on every detail and nuance of the trail I once knew so well. My commuting days have been suspended and often sorely missed since I now work from home.

Carefully lowering my bike off the hooks in my garage, and admiring the new handlebar wraps and tires, both of which had hardly been used, I felt an urge to relive my daily commute. I pumped up the tires, slipped on my biking shoes, then plopped onto my newly replaced bike seat.

Rolling down the driveway, I clipped my shoes into the pedals and pushed forward. I soon realized as I started toward the bike path, it wasn't just the present experience of the bike path that I craved, because the farther I traveled forward, the more the landmarks I rolled by spurred in me nostalgic reflections of my past.

I headed across town and turned left onto Bullocks Point, passing the house which had a lot to do with the start of my biking escapades. It was the house where Mike, my co-worker and friend, lived. One day while carpooling to work together, frustrated by the summer traffic on Route 114 while stuck at a red light, I mentioned almost facetiously that, "It would take less time to ride a bicycle to work than it would to drive."

There are moments in one's life when a subtle, almost whimsical comment, thought, or internal intuition can have a profound effect on one's future. This turned out to be one of those moments, as the idea became the focus of conversation for the remainder of the car ride. After careful consideration during the frustrating commute, a plan was hatched, and at the conclusion of a test ride the following weekend on bicycles we scrounged from family and friends, we had made our decision: this commute would work.

For several seasons, Mike and I made the trip to work together, until his work schedule and logistics did not allow him to continue. He returned to his automotive commute, while I continued to pedal onward. Now, more than twenty years later, Mike and his family have moved back to Bristol. But as I passed the house, the memory that this was where it all began was not lost upon me.

I headed south toward the Looff Carousel, a place where I had spent countless evenings and afternoons with my wife and two daughters when they were young. We would ride the magical creatures that pranced in a circle around the band organ situated in the center of the wooden masterpiece. I wonder if Charles Looff knew when he built this beautiful piece of history at the turn of the century, constructed before my own grandparents were even born, that it would outlive him. It has managed to endure to this very day, and I have no doubt it will outlive me. My family spent numerous occasions dashing for the horses on the perimeter, because for us the calling card of the carousel was the ring dispenser, its contents only attainable by the outstretched arms of the riders situated on the perimeter. The rings became fodder for the clown's mouth that waited patiently at each passing rotation as the music of the organ blared throughout the building. If you were fortunate enough to pull the brass ring from the dispenser, you were awarded a free ride.

Who wouldn't want a chance to capture the brass ring?

I remember when the carousel was part of Crescent Park, a summertime landmark. My parents had taken me there along with my brother and sister on numerous occasions. Often accompanied by other family members, we would spend the day walking the Midway, dining on chowder and clam cakes, and riding the smaller rides while I watched in amazement as the roller coaster carried screaming patrons careening around its gigantic wooden tracks. I always wanted to ride the coaster when I got big enough, but the park closed when I was thirteen, just old enough to muster the courage to undertake such an adventure. The land where Crescent Park resided is now an apartment complex, the carousel being the only remnant that remains.

Memories of the times spent at the park flashed through my mind as I turned left down the aptly named Crescent View Avenue, heading along the waters of Bullocks Cove. My pace was slower than I remembered, and my legs and lungs were suddenly aware of the task at hand. Although resisting slightly, my body persisted onward, winding through the flat expanse of pavement, stopping only at intersections to ensure the cars were granting me the right of way.

As I continued onward along a secluded stretch of pavement, I thought of the benefits the bike path had afforded me during my commuting days. Along with providing me exercise on a regular basis, the money spent on biking clothes and accessories were more than offset by the savings on the cost of gas to and from work. And by the time I rode home — which was required whether I felt like riding or not — any stresses of the day melted away by the melodic, serene cadence of the bike as I made my way through the quiet, lush, and beautiful scenery of the East Bay.

Another advantage of commuting to work on the East Bay bike path was that I was able to experience what neuroscientists call "the default mode." Defined as a network of interacting brain regions that is active when a person is not focused on the outside world, scientists have been analyzing this for years.

Granted, this is the East Bay bike path. The commute is easy and very relaxed. It is not the Pyrenees Mountain range in France where part of the Tour de France takes place. Albeit by the way some people ride the bike path on a Saturday afternoon, dodging fellow bi-pedal occupants as well as strollers and dog-walkers, you would think there was a yellow jersey at stake. The intensity of the ride is less than what professional riders exert, but there's a redundancy of effort and a similarity in focus that produces a type of meditation. The only sounds are from the chain as it catches the gears, the subtle thump of the tires as they pass over the most minute obstacle like a tree branch or a crack in the pavement, or the squeak of the tires compressing and twisting as I take a hard turn. When I ride, there is no radio, no conversation, no interaction or distraction.

My mind is so familiar with the effort required to produce the task that it is afforded the subliminal ability to concentrate and analyze things without even focusing on them. Often, as I rode into work, I could effortlessly concentrate on numerous tasks for any given day down to the smallest detail. Solutions to non-functioning code from the day before would be revealed before I even sat in front of the computer; problems that I had labored under would be unraveled while I labored in the saddle of the bicycle seat. The default mode would kick in, and like a person who discovers a solution to a problem while taking a morning shower, the answers would come to me without a conscious effort. A subliminal mental fortitude would reveal itself without disclosing its source. It was like osmosis for the waking mind, and it was welcomed with open arms.

The only disadvantage to this "default mode" is that often, as I rolled my bike into the building where my office was located, I could barely recollect details of the ride itself. But today there was no office destination, no workload to contemplate. My complete and utter focus was on the path, and the memories that riding it would unveil.

I passed Veterans Field in Barrington, where over the past several years I had laced up my cleats and slipped my hand into my glove to take my spot on the Riverside softball team, where I had played for over fifteen years, a team I still play for today. Veterans Field wasn't our home field — that resided in numerous spots in Riverside over the years — but there were some epic battles that had taken place there, some of which involved team Riverside, and others that did not. All were entertaining, and some were downright intense. As we were a church league, many people questioned the caliber of the players, but those spectators who watched as fly balls made their way out of the park were convinced of the caliber of talent that played in this league.

We won the championship for the first time during the 2020 season. We did not hoist the trophy on the Barrington field per se, but rather in a field across the bay in Cranston. Although the pinnacle of our success was not achieved at Veterans Field, many of the games played there forged the perseverance and athletic aptitude that was needed to make it through that chilly, windy October night in Cranston.

Traversing the bridges that crisscrossed route 114 in Warren, I made my way past the shop where my bike was purchased. The first Christmas after I started my commuting tradition, after proving that I would persist in the endeavor the following spring, my wife and two daughters surprised me with a new bicycle I had taken for a test ride the previous summer. On that fateful Christmas morning, the three girls walked to the neighbor's house where the bike was stored and decorated with a red bow. Their three smiling faces beamed with accomplishment when they wheeled the gift toward the house, and as I watched from the living room window, a smile spread across my face. My wife and children often found it difficult to find things to buy me for Christmas, but that year turned into a bonanza of stress-free shopping for all involved.

That Christmas took place over 25 years ago, and I still ride that same bike today. Often urged over the years by my numerous riding partners to upgrade, I don't think I could ever bear to part with such a prized possession. Having logged thousands and thousands of miles to work and back, plus numerous weekend rides with friends and neighbors, as well as almost a dozen charity rides, some of which consisted of 150 miles over the course of a weekend, my bike and I have seen too many miles, too many roads, and have been part of too many experiences for it to be abandoned. Bicycle newness comes not in the form of replacement, but in upgrades of tires, handle wraps, chains, gear cassettes, and finally, after over twenty years, the original seat after the padding — what little there is of one on a road bike — had worn down to the metal frame. Its sentimental value makes my red steel-framed beauty irreplaceable. Carbon fiber frames, rotary disc brakes, and electronic gear shifters be damned!

I passed the bike shop and headed toward Burrs Hill Park as I continued toward Bristol. After navigating another incline past a building complex to my left, the path became more secluded and the grasses that grew along the sides of the trail became taller, blocking the view to my right. Then suddenly the vegetation cleared, and I detected the scent of salt water as I entered Colt State Park. This was the home of the first bike trail I ever rode on as a kid, when I traveled around the park with my brother, sister, and parents, then as a teenager with my friends.

As I exited the park and continued toward the last section of the trail before it terminated at Independence Park, I was struck by how things had changed in the town where I had grown up. Vanished landmarks that were once hallmarks of the town had been replaced by lesser versions of themselves or, in the worst of cases, torn down completely. I passed the marshes near Poppasquash Road looking out to the right at Narragansett Bay, the aquatic pathway from the docks at the end of State Street out into the Atlantic Ocean. To my right was the waterfront where The Castle Restaurant once stood. A landmark I remember well, and the place my parents celebrated their wedding reception in 1964, it had been gutted and replaced by condominiums. I thought it apropos that my parents outlived the very building where they celebrated their marriage. Crossing an intersection, I passed another such place. The Beach House, which was once Kelly's Hamburgers, a place I barely remember as it was recreated in the mid-70s just as my age hit double digits. The location had also been home to the Agave Restaurant and the Topside Bar, an establishment that was booming during my early twenties, but which also somehow did not survive. Just past the Beach House on the bike trail was a place called The Sandbar Restaurant, which my co-workers and I frequented during lunch before we even started on our bicycle escapades to and from work. The restaurant has also long since disappeared, but my memories of these places remain.

I pedaled into Independence Park, coming to the end of the trail, then continued past it onto Thames Street. Turning left up State Street, I headed right onto 114 in downtown Bristol. Contrary to the places that only existed in my memory, there was one remnant still there, vibrant and visible. There in the middle of the road, painted lines that separated the lanes of the road. Not just two lines, but three. One red, one white, and one blue. Like the three sections of our lives; the past, present, and the future.

The present is the smallest section of the timeline, because hopefully we have had enough opportunity to fill the past with a plethora of experiences, while the future — even more hopefully — contains all the possibilities which still lie ahead of us, as well as the time in which to fulfill those possibilities. Whether or not the lines of our future will be longer than the etches of our past is one of the great mysteries, but it is this unknown that drives us, that propels us to fill our lives with all we possibly can.

Those three lines also represented another landmark of my youth, and of every Bristol resident. For this tradition has outlived the oldest members of the town, and existed longer than the U.S. Railroad Administration, the White House, and the United States Mint. The town legacy I'm talking about is none other than the Fourth of July Parade.

As part of an annual hometown tradition that has been going on for over 250 years, the citizens of Bristol, along with a plethora of visitors who multiply the population of the town for a single day, congregate on the streets of Bristol for an annual event that is the oldest of its kind in the entire United States. I've witnessed this extravaganza for as long as I can remember, and one year I was lucky enough to be a part of it. When I was in my early twenties, I worked as a camp counselor at the local YMCA, another building that was important to my upbringing and a focal point for many of the town's residents before it met its own demise. Some of the pre-teen members of the camp were asked to ride a float, and we, as the camp counselors, were asked to provide supervision. It is quite a different experience traveling the two miles along the parade route riding a float as opposed to witnessing the event sitting on the blankets that my father would lay out on the lawn in front of the sidewalk year after year. It is a perspective I will never forget.

I sometimes wonder if I took the Fourth of July Parade for granted. Some people travel great distances to see the parade, which for me was always within walking distance from my parents' house. Proximity can often be indirectly proportion to appreciation. Do people who live next to the Grand Canyon ever get to the point where, when they wake up, instead of a wondrous gasp at the awesomeness at the sight of the landscape in front of them, they simply stretch and yawn?

Heading south, I pedaled hard and turned right onto Constitution Street, then right again onto Thames Street, the waters of Narragansett Bay gleaming and bright to my left. I headed back to the bike trail, my companion and confidant for so many days — and miles — of my past. Without further reflection, I passed the buildings that had changed from when I knew them in my youth, and as I crossed Poppasquash Road, I relived the memories of the places that had forged the person I had become today. Bristol was no longer the place I lived, or worked, but it would always be the place where I was made. I lifted off the seat and pedaled hard, focusing on the trail below me as the tires hummed along, and I thought of how much time I had spent riding on it over the years.

I caught the bike trail and headed north, reflecting on the lost aspects of the town that now only existed in my memory. Places that were important to me had disappeared, while others still clung to life, and although I did not visit them as often as I did when I lived and worked in Bristol, these places still resonated within me. Ball fields and parks, diners and restaurants, buildings that held special memories not only for myself, but for my family, and I'm sure, other residents of Bristol as well. For me, all these impressions were intertwined by the path upon which I was riding, and as I headed out of town, I realized that it was this path, this repaved railroad track turned into a pedestrian landmark in the smallest state of the union, that lead me back to my childhood home.

ↀ

**Kevin Duarte** first had a poem published in his college's anthology when he was a senior. In his late twenties, a local company produced a comic book called "P.R.I.M.E." which Kevin wrote with a friend. The comic was produced and sold well in the local area. The story of the book's publication even garnered local TV coverage.

His thriller novel, *Flashpoint*, has been submitted to agents, and *Manifest Destiny* is now in its final draft phase. Kevin's third novel, *The Zemeckis Theorem*, is the first book in a series, *The Quantum Children*, and currently in the works.

Kevin enjoys writing speculative science fiction as well as fantasy. He is inspired by the possibilities of the human collective, both good and bad, and he loves to create characters as much as he enjoys creating and modifying the world around them.

# ORDER FORM

Please use the following to order additional copies of

*Hope* (2020), *Past, Present & Future* (2019), *Selections (2018), Under the 13th Star* (2017), and/or *Shoreline* (2016),
Selected Short Fiction, Nonfiction, Poetry and Prose from The Association of Rhode Island Authors

| | (QTY) | | | | |
|---|---|---|---|---|---|
| _____ | (QTY) | **Iconic Rhode Island** | X | $10.00 Total $ _____ |
| _____ | (QTY) | **Green** | X | $10.00 Total $ _____ |
| _____ | (QTY) | **Hope** | X | $10.00 Total $ _____ |
| _____ | (QTY) | **Past, Present, and Future** | X | $10.00 Total $ _____ |
| _____ | (QTY) | **Selections** | X | $15.00 Total $ _____ |
| _____ | (QTY) | **Under the 13th Star** | X | $10.00 Total $ _____ |
| _____ | (QTY) | **Shoreline** | X | $10.00 Total $ _____ |

**Shipping & Handling $ _____

GRAND TOTAL $ _____

**Shipping & Handling: Please add $3.00 for the first copy, and $1.50 for each additional copy.

Payment Method:

___ Personal Check Enclosed (Payable to ARIA)

___ Charge my Credit Card

Name: _____ BILLING ZIP CODE: _____

Visa____ MC_____ Amex_____ Discover____

Card Number: _____ EXP: _____ / _____ CSC _____

Signature: _____

Ship To:

Name _____

Street _____

City _____ State: _____ Zip: _____

Phone _____ Email: _____

___ Check to add to ARIA's email list.

MAIL YOUR COMPLETED FORM TO:
**The Association of Rhode Island Authors (ARIA)**
**c/o Stillwater Books**
**175 Main St.**
**Pawtucket, RI 02860**
info@stillwaterpress.com
www.StillwaterPress.com
www.RIAuthors.org

Made in United States
North Haven, CT
05 August 2022

22273657R00108